Mudrooroo was born in Narrogin, Western Australia in 1938 and has since travelled extensively throughout Australia and the world. Mudrooroo is active in Aboriginal cultural affairs. He is a member of the Aboriginal Arts Unit committee of the Australia Council, and was a co-founder with Jack Davis of the Aboriginal Writers, Oral Literature and Dramatists' Association. He has also piloted Aboriginal literature courses at Murdoch University, the University of Queensland, the University of the Northern Territory and Bond University. Mudrooroo is a prolific writer of poetry, prose and criticism. His most recent novel was *Master of the Ghost Dreaming*. At present he is working on a new novel set in India where he lived for seven years, three as a Buddhist monk.

Also by Mudrooroo
and available in Imprint

MASTER OF THE GHOST DREAMING

IMPRINT CLASSICS

# WILD CAT FALLING

## COLIN JOHNSON
## MUDROOROO

*Introduced by*
*Stephen Muecke*

Angus&Robertson
An imprint of HarperCollins*Publishers*

AN ANGUS & ROBERTSON BOOK
An imprint of HarperCollinsPublishers

First published in Australia in 1965 by Angus & Robertson Publishers
Sirius Quality Paperback edition first published in 1979
Reprinted 1984 (three times), 1987 (three times), 1990
This Imprint Classic edition published in 1992
Reprinted in 1992 by
CollinsAngus&Robertson Publishers Pty Limited (ACN 009 913 517)
A division of HarperCollinsPublishers (Australia) Pty Limited
25 Ryde Road, Pymble NSW 2073, Australia

HarperCollinsPublishers (New Zealand) Limited
31 View Road, Glenfield, Auckland 10, New Zealand

HarperCollinsPublishers Limited
77–85 Fulham Palace Road, London W6 8JB, United Kingdom

Copyright © Mudrooroo 1965
          © In introduction Stephen Muecke 1992

National Library of Australia
Cataloguing-in-Publication data:

Nyoongah, Mudrooroo, 1939–  .
    Wild cat falling

    ISBN 0 207 17446 6.

    1. Title.

A823.3

Cover image taken from the original 1965 edition
Printed in Australia by Griffin Paperbacks, Adelaide

5 4 3 2
95 94 93 92

# INTRODUCTION

'A friend always leaves a track —
this is the teaching of the Aborigines.'
David Unaipon

It was in 1965 that Mudrooroo put down tracks in this, the
first novel by an Aboriginal Australian. Writing can be a
generous and friendly gesture (because it makes communi-
cation an instructive pleasure), but for Mudrooroo it was
also a struggle, just to get his book out. His tracks are still
here, for you to follow them up and to see which way he was
going then, or even which way Australia was going then, es-
pecially in terms of its treatment of the Aboriginal peoples.

Mudrooroo was born in 1938 when Australia was coming
out of a depression and going into a war. In Western
Australia Aboriginal people were largely invisible, and
being forced onto missions. The prevailing attitude was
summed up by the title of Daisy Bates' influential book, also
of 1938, *The Passing of the Aborigines*. Mudrooroo was born
into a society where assimilation was the government policy,
and many of his people were surviving by forgetting their
traditions as quickly as possible. This book emerged as a
quite radical text, with a story which goes against this prevailing attitude, even before radicalism became fashionable
in the late sixties and seventies, it was only in 1972 that the
Aboriginal Tent Embassy in Canberra became a symbol of
an emergent Australian Black consciousness.

Why did it take so long for Aboriginal Australia to produce a novel? Kath Walker's (Oodgeroo Noonucal) poetry
made a splash about the same time, other people had been
writing ever since David Unaipon first went to print in the
1920s in South Australia. But Mudrooroo's novel was
unique in that it made a leap not only as a piece of writing

which was radical politically, but also as a radical genre.

It was radical in this sense because the novel was about the furthest one could move away from traditional Aboriginal genres. Drama was closer to the 'corroboree', poetry was closer to song, and oral narrative closer to the short story than the novel was to anything Aboriginal. It is perhaps for this reason that Mudrooroo was later to write an important critical essay called 'White Form, Aboriginal Content' and then move on to experimental writing in more synthetic (in the sense of mixed) genres, like *Doin' Wildcat: a Novel Koori Script* (1988).

So it was not, of course, a lack of civilisation which stopped Aborigines from writing books. Writing does not *equal* civilisation, and many oral traditions are still in place, providing a point of coherence and a confidence in traditional culture. There has been a suspicion of the book, of what the written word represents in terms of, say, the law. Aborigines have long been apprehensive about European education and in many ways have found it difficult to distinguish from prison — the disciplinary regimes can be much the same. Traditional Aboriginal education does not work in the same way as European education. For a start it happens in conjunction with a nomadic lifestyle, with moving around and learning a hunter-gatherer economy. And just as in all cultures, the liveliness and warmth of the spoken word ensures the survival of a culture. Books are for different purposes, mass-market commodities, the tools of education, and so on. To the extent that they are unfamiliar artifacts in Aboriginal culture, the young Colin Johnson had quite a few prejudices to overcome. But I think that one thing that helped him was that he came to have a confidence in the notion of the artist as a kind of outcast from society, and it was in this way that he was able to create a structural parallel to run the motor of his novel, with the figure of the Black and beatnik artist as doubly outcast, in the form of his nameless hero.

But before I 'introduce' the novel I should discuss the

foreword which has been travelling with the novel ever since it was first published. It is long and prominently placed. Not all novels have to be introduced in such a long and compromising manner. What is the function of things like forewords, prefaces, introductions? If the main text cannot speak for itself, why isn't it rewritten? forewords are written by prominent people to endorse the application of an unknown person to enter 'society'. They are texts which smooth the passage of the unknown text. If, as I said before, the main text is politically strange or unsettling, then the foreword will have the function of ensuring that such contradictions are smoothed over. They are part of the packaging, like the dust jacket of the original edition which had a modernist image of a lanky dark figure shuffling down the wet city streets, slashed across with a red wraparound endorsement from Colin Simpson: 'A breakthrough in Australian writing — by the first young intellectual of aboriginal blood . . . an ex-bodgie . . . His talent could rock you with its charge of promise.' But *my* Introduction is different, Mudrooroo now 'needs no introduction', mine is a commentary coming at the end of a long line of commentary around the work of a writer who is as well known in France and Denmark as he is in Australia.

So in the novel itself, the main character is not given a name. There might be two aspects to this. One is that it expresses the alienation of the character, his marginality in white society. Not to have a name is to be unplaced. The other aspect is one from Aboriginal culture where people often don't address each other by given names, but by kinship names (Mum, Uncle, etc.) or by descriptions. For instance, the following exchange establishes these points:

> 'Good day, Mum. Just got out of bloody, stinking jail.'
> 'I knew you were in, son,' she says, 'Making quite a name for yourself.'
> 'How did you know?' I ask. 'I thought they didn't publish the juvenile names.'

'Your friend came and told me.'

'What friend?'

'That pimply-faced boy.'

'He's an acquaintance. I don't have any friends.' (pp. 111–112)

The story is divided up into a number of parts, mostly consisting of flashbacks. The main story — about a young man who is released from jail, meets up with two groups of people, his former bodgie friends and the white achieving middle-class university set, then steals a car with a friend, shoots a policeman and is arrested again — is interspersed with episodes from his past which progressively provide the background for his current story.

Important in this background is his mother and her Aboriginal relatives. It is the mother who is there when he has his 'wild cat falling' nightmare, and it is her uncle, the old wandering rabbiter, who explains that the wild cat is some sort of tribal totem, or something more like a tribal memory which he has to try to recover.

Significantly, the main character is unable to come to terms with his love of or connection with his mother, he tries to be 'tough', just as she has tried to reject her own Aboriginal background (the assimilationist policy again, but eventually she does go back to her own people). This inability to connect with the mother has its repercussions in the hero's relations with women. Every time he makes love, or wants to, all he seems to notice is breasts and nipples, then he is sick, or is full of remorse. It is no accident that I make this crude psychoanalytic reading, the notion of the unconscious, the dream, is the key to the origin of the title, without necessarily making yet another crude connection, to the Aboriginal notion of 'the Dreaming'.

But if the 'wild cat' dream is to be related to the Aboriginal notion of 'dreaming' then this is only to the extent that there is a spiritual heritage in certain texts (songs and stories) which are *unconsciously* passed from one generation to another. In a double movement, the hero also links the dream with a fall he had as a child. The Western psycho-analytic reading tempts us to search for explanations located in traumatic childhood experience so that here, then, the 'truth' of Aboriginality is collapsed into the 'truth' of the psyche. The formation of personality in trauma and repression is a very familiar story, but here it is linked with Aboriginal political trauma, the forgetting of history. This key passage makes the novel one of the most economic and powerful statements in the history of Australian literature.

But there is more. The elements of the dream are also constructed as an allegory of the boy's contemporary condition — part-Aboriginal (Crow), part-European (Cat), both black (like the clothes he wears), attempting to fly, which is like a symbol of escape, achievement, or even love, but he is destined to crash to earth, like the wax-winged Icarus who tried to fly too close to the sun in the classical story.

The fact that this story is revealed by the old Aboriginal man is a sign that the cultural momentum of the book points towards revival, a searching for roots, and the maintenance of links between contemporary Aboriginal Australia and traditional Aboriginal Australia. In the novelist's social context he had to assert this kind of story against the prevailing policy, and one can only imagine how difficult this must have been, and how it prefigured the radicalism which was to come later. In a different situation the novel might just as easily have been written in terms of the successful assimilation of the young black to white society, he could have gone off with June, the white student who attracted him. But we can reject this possibility as soon as we bring it up. That story would not have worked for reasons of both content and form.

Formally, the novel sets up from the start the cyclical idea of *return* (remember the Contents page has the titles: Foreword, One: Release, Two: Freedom, Three: Return). The Freedom episode deals with the *possibility* of his relationship with June, from meeting her on the beach to the party with the students, but we know that the story, in terms of structure, has to end up where it began.

And in terms of *content*, an assimilationist novel would have been a betrayal of Aboriginality, and of marginality. It might also have been political suicide for the author. There is an aesthetic of marginality involved here. The Aboriginality can be linked up with the French existentialist writers (Camus, Sartre, Beckett). It is a romance of solitude in an absurd world; the only way to go is out from the social centre, away from suburban life towards the dark regions of the individual soul where creativity is supposed to lie. The artist has to be alone, responsible only to himself, but pulled into the world of people by chance encounters (June, Denise, Jeff) and by the gun going off in a moment of panic. If you read that passage again it's quite like the 'chance' killing in Albert Camus' *The Outsider* (an influential book at the time Johnson was writing):

> The torch beam swings and slaps me full in the face. I blink and panic and the rifle explodes with a crack of doom into the blinding light. (pp. 115–116)

This character is not self-motivated — things just happen to him. This is a novel more — on the surface — about *indifference* than moral direction, and that indifference lies both in the 'empty' character and in the structure of the social world that produces the indifference.

But this does not mean that the book does not have a lot to say along the way. It says a lot about undoing some of the blatantly racist and more benignly liberal ideas about Aborigines. Particularly impressive is the ironic treatment of the liberal university student on p. 80:

> 'What I always think,' she comes in, 'it's not the natives need educating so much. It's the whites.'
>
> I guess from the way she looks at me that this is the closest she ever got to an Aboriginal. She offers me this chewed old bit of white corn as though expecting me to

seize on it with pleased surprise. How broadminded, how perceptive to express a big, brave thought like that!

The cultural landscape of Perth is drawn out of recent history, like in no other novel, except perhaps *The Delinquents* by Criena Rohan. Our hero is the 'Progressive Dresser' and he belongs to and uses the terminology (sometimes American) of the 'milk-bar bodgie' culture. This intersects (via Jazz) with the culture of the students. But they are in the business of *contemplating* culture — commenting on paintings, Jazz, philosophy and other cultures. And the hero's world is one of *action* as opposed to the world of talk. For the novel this allows Mudrooroo to both 'put ideas in' — those of the 'contemplative' middle-class students plus his critique of them as 'phony' — and to have the action parts of the narrative play themselves out in the street and on the road.

Up ahead the tracks are waiting for you to follow, the Black Words on the White Page, to borrow another critic's phrase. If you couldn't see Mudrooroo's tracks, you might have to take further advice from David Unaipon, whose hero, Narroondarie, feared an enemy. He goes on: 'So he thought to himself, like all wise men do, that he would always be on the alert; and all that day he was not seen.'

So, dear Reader — alert, wise, invisible (and nameless) reader, please remember, when you read the words of *Wild Cat Falling*, that you are following the tracks of a friend.

STEPHEN MUECKE
Sydney, 1992

# FOREWORD

WHEN Colin Johnson left Western Australia for Victoria early in 1958 it seemed hardly likely that he was to become the subject of a curious success story. We saw him off at the Perth railway station, a long, lonely streak of a youth in black jeans, black shirt and flapping overcoat, playing down his apprehension of the big strange city on the other side of the continent. He was nineteen years old and part Aboriginal, though his features would not have betrayed him and his skin colour was no darker than that of a southern European.

At the time he professed to know little and care less about his indigenous heritage. He had tried, in fact, by seeking white companions, to remove himself from the shadow of the native dilemma, and yet it lay upon him as heavily as upon the rest of them. It had darkened his youth and was driving him now, against his every natural instinct, into alien territory where whiteman letters of introduction did not guarantee hospitality as had the message sticks of his Aboriginal ancestors.

These forbears had been members of the big Bibbulmun tribe whose boundaries embraced the fertile south-western triangle from Jurien Bay, 120 miles north of Perth, to the southern port of Esperance and

which, in 1829, had welcomed the first white settlers
as the spirits of their dead returned.

On the west coast both newcomers and Aborigines
made sincere efforts to come to terms, but the end
results were much the same as in other Australian
colonies where the races engaged in mutual hostility.
By the end of the century the tribe had more or less
disappeared, leaving a people of mixed white and
native blood. Some became assimilated into the white
community, but the majority continued to breed
among themselves or back into the Aborigines from
other parts of the State, resulting in a drifting coloured
minority caught in the vicious circle of a lack of opportunity and their own lack of stamina.

The situation that had developed over the years is
shown in the circumstances indirectly responsible for
my meeting with the writer of this book. These concerned a group of south-western Aboriginal children
whose distinctive art work, produced under the inspir-
ation of their teacher, Mr Noel White, had been suc-
cessfully exhibited both at home and abroad. The
demand created for the young people's work gave
them an incentive and prestige that augered well
their future and that, it was hoped, would draw attention to the lack of opportunity offered to many such
naturally gifted children. Instead it was turned to their
disadvantage. The publicity drew attention to the
conditions in which they lived and the Department
of Native Welfare, embarrassed by lack of funds
and staff problems, closed the settlement pending its
transfer to a private missionary body. In the interim

the children became scattered, mostly returning to the outskirt camps of their relatives.

I had previously collaborated with Mrs Florence Rutter, staunch friend and promoter of the young artists' work, in a book* telling something of their background and the development of their talent. After their dispersal, their former teachers and a few other friends had tried to keep in touch with the youngsters, help find steady jobs for them, and encourage them to continue with their art work. Many of the girls, however, drifted into prostitution, the boys into casual or itinerant labouring jobs on farms, timber mills, orchards, or on vineyards where, in fact, they received part payment in wine. Before long most of them had served prison sentences on minor charges of drinking, receiving liquor for their elders,† or petty theft. From first offences that, in the case of white boys and girls, would have been dismissed as mere peccadilloes, it became very difficult for them to avoid being returned to jail. They were constantly under the surveillance of the police, some sympathetic and helpful, others seeking native convictions as easy stepping-stones to promotion.

Early in 1958, I was asked to find accommodation for a boy who was coming to a job in the city. I expected to see one of the youths we knew but he turned out to be a complete stranger with little of the familiar coloured boy's willing-to-please manner. In

*The Child Artists of the Australian Bush: Harrap.

† By the middle of 1964 major citizenship rights, including the franchise and the freedom to drink alcohol were granted to all natives in every State except Queensland, where legislation is still under review.

fact he showed little obvious trace of native blood, but he had, what most of the darker people have lost, the proud stance and sinuous carriage of the tall, tribal Aboriginal.

As it turned out the "someone" who had promised him the job had regretted the impulse and it did not materialize. Other contacts had likewise grown wary of coloured boys and Colin did not go out of his way to ingratiate himself with prospective employers. "Who knows?" he would retort, when asked whether he would diligently apply himself to a job in question. It was a sort of last ditch stand for his right as an individual to speak the truth as he knew it, no more and no less. How, in fact, *could* he guarantee he would stick a job of which he had no experience? "Why not?" he would ask of a suggestion to which he could express no immediate objection. It was an honest enough question and left it up to you.

We gathered that Colin had been born in the farming town of Narrogin, 120 miles from Perth, in 1938. His mother belonged to that district and he had brothers and sisters scattered about the State. He had never known his father, who had died soon after he was born. He had been baptized a Catholic but had since dismissed all Christian denominations as hypocritical. In the process of a broken education, partly acquired in an orphanage, he had attained his Junior Public certificate, a qualification all too rare among coloured youths. He had at some stage belonged to a Bodgie group, but although he clung to their mode of dress he had finally rejected this cult as beneath his intelligence.

At the time of our meeting he had hoped to get a city job and study for his matriculation at night school. This seemed well within his capabilities, for we soon realized that, from whatever odd combination of genes and circumstance, the boy was a natural intellectual. He was an omnivorous reader and had somehow acquired a surprising general knowledge of the classics and more than a smattering of psychology, philosophy and comparative religions. He was also interested in drama, art and music—particularly jazz. His hunger for knowledge was matched with a retentive memory that my own children were quick to exploit —one of them to provide points for an inter-school debate on the merits and demerits of automation.

An above average I.Q. could, however, have been more burden than advantage had he inherited the typical instability of the out-camp people. We observed that Colin was not apparently lazy. He found jobs for himself about the place and did them well. He also had a sense of time and he began to seem— was it possible?—even dependable.

He had hardened himself to expect failure and rebuffs but had none the less enough conceit of himself to believe that he could somewhere make his mark if given an ordinary chance. Before long he had the offer of a steady clerical job, but he now had his doubts about living in Perth. Some of his former associates had got into trouble and it was difficult, in a small city, to avoid running into them under the watchful eye of the law.

An alternative was offered by the Reverend Stan Davey of the Aboriginal Advancement League in Victoria, who had helped many young people similarly placed to find jobs in Melbourne.

"Why not?" Colin asked, when the proposition was put to him. Melbourne would be sink or swim—a genuine test of stamina.

Despite the confidence we had in him, it was not without misgivings that we watched his train move off. It might have been to his advantage had he been more conspicuously of native blood and with more of the endearing Aboriginal trustfulness and obvious will to please. Would the people "over there" have time in their busy lives to recognize the qualities we had found under his veneer of toughness and indifference? Would he now disappear, to be next heard of in jail as other young friends had done despite protestations of faithfulness and promises to go straight? Somehow we thought not, although Colin had protested nothing. He had not, I think, even promised to write.

Before long we received a letter describing his journey, his quite unexpected, perhaps Aboriginal, reaction to the desert, and his impressions of Melbourne. A little later he returned the money for his fare and basic equipment and thereafter continued writing at fairly regular intervals, telling about his job in a filing department, his attendance at night school, and his continuing search for some truth that would be "valid" for himself. He began attending Buddhist meetings which impressed him so much that he decided to "give up meat for ever", along with Rock-and-Roll and ballet. However tempted towards these pleasures, "*Mara*," he wrote, "*shall not prevail.*"

It was mooted that he might go to Burma to become a monk and in the process of inquiries he was presented with a life of Gautama Buddha by the Burmese consul. Meanwhile he continued his ordinary studies, but with Buddhism and Yoga in ascendancy. "How wonderful," he exclaimed, "to escape from dreary civilization into sweet nothingness!"

On brief holidays he discovered the lush beauty of the Dandenongs, camped, read and luxuriated in a landscape "where, between two breasts of green a township rests serene as a child in its mother's arms and ferns and undergrowth creep up over roads and clearings. . . . When the wind blows up, the trees moan and groan in a sort of agony of joy and here and there a dead gum stretches ghostly arms to the sky as if praying for life again. The air is full of the sounds of birds and insects exulting to be alive and free, and of a milky stream that hurry-hurries down the valley. . . ."

Early in 1959 he was asked to go as a Western Australian delegate to a Federal conference of the Aboriginal Advancement League. "I did," he told us, "but sat there too chicken to do anything. . . . I was a failure, but I enjoyed the meetings as they gave me an insight into what is being done to elevate and to obtain citizen rights for my people."

About the same time he wrote of going to hear Billy Graham.

> It was rather terrifying to see how so many people (including myself) can be influenced emotionally by a voice, a choir and their own fears. . . .

After a longer silence than usual he wrote, in November 1959:

> Time has pried loose a few months of my life and I cannot tell what he has done with them. . . .
>
> I am a Bohemian type now. Well, not exactly that but a Beatnik engaged in the Holy Search for Self. I have grown a small beard and wander vaguely through Melbourne just looking and looking, thinking and thinking. . . .
>
> But I still listen to music. I go to classical concerts now and appreciate them, but I also still feel Rock and Roll and Jazz, and dance and sway to them. I can be moved with the Blues and cry with the Negroes of old.
>
> I also like Art. I go to exhibitions and know some of Melbourne's Bohemians and Intellectuals. So you see my mind has been broadened a bit, or so I hope. . . . At the moment I am out of a job, being typical Beatnik, but I have written a play called "The Delinks".

I did not read the play, but he sent me some poems written about this time. They were somewhat cliché ridden expositions of Beatnik philosophy in which people were "immersed in shadows and nothingness", bent under a "leaden weight of sorrow", wondering whether the world had ever been young and gay, the trees green instead of blue and the moon "a yellow orb of serenity". This conformity of outlook held in check for a while the original expression of which he was capable, but to have made a creative effort of any sort was at least some departure from the nihilism that had previously absorbed him.

When the University quarterly *Westerly* announced a competition for stories or sketches by people of Aboriginal blood I suggested that he enter something written from his own experience or observation. He sent two sketches, one of a boy whiling away some dreary hours in a down-town Melbourne night club (very Beatnik), and another the feelings of a boy on the morning of his release from jail. The latter, he said, was part of a novel he intended working on.

Entries in the competition were foreseeably few, but in any case Colin's starkly telling little sketch would have found its way to the top. Encouraged by his win, he set himself seriously to writing his novel, on which he sent occasional progress reports.

The book concerns a part Aboriginal boy trying to find himself and failing . . . a sort of mock hero, a stupid, self-pitying, broken-down mess, barely existing. He is *not myself*, though a little perhaps what I might have turned out. He talks and acts like many delinquents I have observed and I have put into his mind some of my own doubts and foolish contradictions. I'm afraid it is pretty dreary and uneven. . . .

.    .    .    .    .

I lead a mere, vague, bumbling existence now, broken by frenzied spells of writing. At night when I am working it sounds all right. By daylight I know that my glorious novel is *bad*. Sometimes I get quite disgusted with it and don't care if it is lost or destroyed. I tell myself however that I am just lazy, as most primitive people are supposed to be, and that when I see hard work ahead I want to disappear. Then I come back, look again and get enmeshed in it once more.

.    .    .    .    .

I think style is my main difficulty—the smooth connection of sentences and images, the switching from subjective to objective points of view. . . . I am going about seeking dialogue these days, examining people's words and also going to plays for this purpose. . . .

.    .    .    .    .

Thanks for your criticism of the section forwarded. I wanted the book to be a sort of *Pilgrim's Progress* rather than a particular person beset with his own separate problems, but I can see I have not brought this off. I am therefore making my character more positive in tone and altering his outlook a little, while keeping his ambiguities, false thinking and contradictions. . . . He must continue to reject life, shoulders slouched, head low, hands in pockets, shuffling. . . .

Yes, I will prune because I see it is necessary, but about the repetitions—Aboriginal poetry and songs are full of them and so are the French writers—the neo-realists. . . . Perhaps I am too much under the influence of the Existentialists and the French school of abstract aloneness or whatever of Beckett, Sartre, Robbé Gillet and the rest. I realize I tend to imitate them and am getting myself out of this. Still, I excuse myself by saying (even if it's not valid) that I am young and Australian and most of them are old and European and therefore my findings must be different. . . . One point I want to stress is that the character I portray is not against the world—he thinks the world is against *him*. I consider this important because it shows that he is not a juvenile dramatizing his condition, but rather that his faulty perception of the world causes him to dramatize it. In *The Catcher In the Rye* the position is reversed. . . .

Unfortunately—or could it be otherwise?—I feel very detached from what they call "The Australian Way of Life". Australianisms seem false and meaningless to me— "fair dinkum" they do, but I "dig" the beatnik jargon. It comes naturally. . . .

I now agree with you about repetition. It does get boring except where skilfully used for some deliberate effect. But you know about muddled sentences—I dote on them, but I realize that no one else will. I like your last sentence and must quote it some time: "Contradictions are all right so long as the reader does not suspect it is the *writer's* mind that is in a stew."

These extracts indicate the seriousness with which Colin had come to regard the writer's craft and the extraordinary patience and tenacity with which he was applying himself to it. His life apart from the job to which he soon returned, continued meanwhile as a persistent search for a personal truth among the religions, cults and arts of East and West. Curiosity led him inevitably into so many odd associations that I wondered at times whether after all his *Mara* might win the day. His letters were disturbingly frank and to the point, but I need not have feared for him. He emerged from each new experience with another set of questions and a further mental horizon:

> Does merging with the infinite result in identity or loss of identity? Is identity equal to personality or to something else? In all my reading I find that the words used to express this thing are much the same, with minor differences due to differing cultural groups and languages. I have yet myself to find a meaning in life. At the moment it seems to have nothing to offer me, except perhaps records. . . . I spend my wages on jazz, folksong and blues and my time reading science fiction, poetry, Hindu philosophy and plays. . . .

His attraction to Buddhism and Indian philosophy may have been some equation of Eastern mysticism to that of the Aboriginal *Dreaming* in which he became increasingly interested.

"I now find myself oriented to the Aboriginal people," he wrote, "and am for the first time definitely committed to a race."

He attended meetings concerned with Aboriginal advancement and collected signatures for a petition for the removal of discriminatory clauses from the law. He also became implicated with a dance group

". . . formed for the purpose of bringing Aboriginal culture—mainly dancing—before an audience and thus laying the foundation for a purely Australian art form."

When the Aborigines, collected from goodness knows where, "went to jail or wandered away", Colin and his associates in the venture planned to gather a number of tribal-living natives from Western Australia and set them up in Melbourne as "professors" of a true Australian culture. This foredoomed experiment, however, soon died a natural death.

He began moving in left-wing political circles, attending ban-the-bomb meetings and adopting "a Marxist attitude to society", but he does not seem to have got very deeply involved. Before long he wrote:

> Can't stand the middle class, the workers, or the Beatniks any more. Went to a working class party and drank and nothing else. Was flung out of a lower middle class party for sneering. Went to a Beatnik party and drank a bit and talked, which was somewhat better. . . . If one works with and knows people one has to drink with them or snub them—especially around Christmas time. . . . I have now taken up learning the guitar, the first really new interest I have had in ages. . . .

During this period he wrote me that he had become acquainted with the author Criena Rohan who encouraged his writing and whose untimely death, after the publication of her novel *The Delinquents*, deprived him of one of the few people with whom he could discuss his work.

In the meantime he had sent me his completed M.S. which I showed to my friend, the writer and literary critic, Florence James, then on a visit to Australia. She agreed with me that it was a first novel of unusual promise and significance, but that it was still in need of some organization. We had both been engaged to talk at a writers' school in Adelaide, so Colin hitchhiked from Melbourne to join us there and to discuss final editing. By this time, however, he was more interested in talking over ideas for further books and seemed to regard *Wild Cat Falling* somewhat in the light of an exercise or a proof of staying power—a deflection, perhaps, of the pointed bone of his Aboriginal heritage.

To his surprise, but not to ours, we soon found a publisher who believed with us that the book was important, both for its literary quality and as the first attempt by someone of Aboriginal blood to express himself in this form. The writer's use of the first person and the realism of his portrayal should not lead the reader to identify him with the details of his story. The book should be read as a work of fiction by a young man who, although open to the degenerate influences of native camps and milk bar gangs, has been strong enough to set himself a positive goal requiring detachment and discipline. The honesty of his approach floodlights a sinister and dangerously expanding area of the post-war world that few outsiders can begin to understand. His "make-believe-they-are-alive-kids", convinced that they have plumbed experience and added up the sum of life, haunt a juke-box limbo of abysmal boredom, their only aim to flout accepted morals and behaviour and to provide themselves by theft and violence with the ritual trappings of their cult. The author has allowed himself no sentimentality; he has made no overt attempt to enlist the reader's sympathy for the "mock-hero" who baffles and exasperates even those most concerned for his welfare. None the less, the story is an unconscious appeal and an imperative challenge to the society that breeds his kind.

*Western Australia*
*December 1964*                                    MARY DURACK

# CONTENTS

I

RELEASE

*page 1*

II

FREEDOM

*page 27*

III

RETURN

*page 95*

# I
# RELEASE

# one

TODAY the end and the gates will swing to eject me, alone and so-called free. Another debt paid to society and I never owed it a thing. Going outside into the fake heaven I have dreamed of these last eighteen months. Lifetime lousy months. Lifetime boredom of sameness. Same people, same talk, sick sameness of dirty jokes. Same sick sagas of old jobs pulled and new jobs planned. Heroic memories. Swell hopes.

Nearly eleven o'clock and ready for the shower that will clean our prison-fouled bodies for the sweet fresh air of the free world. A screw stands by as we file in. The stalls are waist high to prevent prisoners breaking rules. No talking. No sex. Today he lets up on the talking ban and stands blank-eyed, uninterested. No one would dream of breaking any other rule on the last day. Except possibly myself.

For me Fremantle jail has been a refuge of a sort. They have accepted me here as I have accepted hopelessness and futility. The others still have their hopes. Some even make resolutions—but they will fail and fall. Out a few weeks or days, then back a few years in jail sweet jail. Hope is an illusion for squares. I don't fall for it. Don't care any more. I trained myself this way so no phoney emotion can touch me. I go through the actions of life, like in a dream. Actor and audience. Split personality. I can get outside my skin and look at myself.

I stand aside and see myself now, grinning stupidly as I soap my long, lean body. Today the shower is hot for a change and the jets trickle soothingly over my skin. Mother's hands faked by memory. The hissing water becomes her voice, "There, there. Everything will be all right." Phoney comfort. Has anything ever been all right?

Let the water be a girl's hands. Soft like in romantic novels—
> Love me tender, love me long.
> All my dreams come true. . . .

Mother love, boy-girl love—all love is fantasy. Taking a busty woman to bed and done with it like in the gaudy paper-backs they smuggle in here. That's enough I guess. Like I mean, that's life.

I listen to the other cons making with the patter—kidding each other about the great things they're going to do to celebrate release. Some look uneasy just the same, secretly scared to face the world again. With me it's not so much that I'm scared, I only know it will be worse out there. What's to do but lie about in some cheap room until I can't stand it any longer, and then meet up with the milk-bar gang again? Green light on the road home to jail.

I remember that first time in. Sixteen years old and standing sick and scared in the corridor wishing I was dead. How huge the place seemed. Four tiers of cells reaching to the ceiling and daylight greying in through the dirty skylight. A centre space where the cons lined up to be marched off to work, to be fed or locked up again. The cells square, small, with white-washed walls and highly polished floors containing a bed, stool, table bolted to the floor, and a shit bucket. Bare electric bulb watching balefully. All ugly and desolate as hell. It is ugly still, but so familiar now I hardly notice it.

The social classes are rigid here. Screws the contemptible masters, tough cons the bosses next in line, stool pigeons the outcasts. The rest a formless mass, neither big nor small, only there. It is more clear cut than outside and I soon found out who to trust and mix with and who to avoid. Summed it up pretty quickly and decided to make my mark.

The screw was an ex-army type turned warder. Real neat. Tidy moustache, highly polished shoes, never missing a chance to show off his medals. He was in charge of the Juvenile Section, a tough mob trying to talk and act like they thought criminals should. Like gangsters in American movies. You had to be extra tough to make your way up with them.

This day I was supposed to take round the bucket of tea and fill the mugs outside the cell doors. I picked the bucket up, put it down again on the floor and folded my arms.

"You there! Pick up that bucket," the warder roared in his best parade ground voice. "Hop to it!"

I took a long look at him and sneered back in my best Hollywood crim voice: "Who do you think

5

you're ordering around, you little animal? Do it your bloody self."

Then I jerked up the bucket and flung the tea in his face. Tough screw, now wet little man, whipped out his whistle and blew a chorus of hysterical shrieks. Help arrived and the episode ended with the struggling offender being dragged off. . . .

The prison magistrate and superintendent sat at a desk in judgment.

"You are charged with assault, with disobeying orders, and insolence to an officer How do you plead?"

"I don't know."

"Guilty or not guilty?"

"I don't know."

"Take that insolent grin off your face and plead."

Grin faded. Spirit collapsed. "Guilty."

"You are sentenced to fourteen days solitary confinement. Seven days bread and water."

I was led away between two warders. We marched across the main division to a door. One screw juggled with the lock and we marched through. First screw waited to lock up again and the other took the lead. We went through an iron gate and into an enclosure with a three-foot margin between wall and building. A box within a box. Flat, grey concrete roof and square windows spaced at uniform intervals and divided by bars into smaller squares.

We entered the building and stood in a long passage with doors fast locked on either side. The key scraped. One door opened to reveal another. Double doors to give a complete feeling of isolation.

"Undress, you!"

The cold air struck my skin and I stood shivering and goose-pimpled while the screw searched my clothes and flung them into the cell.

"Come on you. Up here."

He watched intently as I took a rug and mattress from an empty cell.

"Leave them between the doors."

I did as commanded and entered the cell. The inner door clanged shut and the outer one gave a muffled thud as it closed. I was alone.

I put on my clothes and sat on the hard, bare floor. There was light enough from the small, high window to read the Bible that was the only other thing in the cell besides a bucket.

Days and nights drifted and merged. In the morning I received a quarter of a loaf of bread and a mug of water. In the evening the same. I saw only two people during this time—the warder on duty and the con who emptied the bucket. All day it was cold and I huddled in the corner and read.

The nights were better. At the time of the evening's bread and water I brought the blanket and mattress into the cell. Between window and door there was enough room to stretch out, and after a while I could get warm and sleep.

Time continued its cold and warm drifting. When I finished the Bible there was nothing to do but lie on my back and let my mind wander and my eyes rove. I stared at the ceiling, white and remote, at the wooden floor, cold and splintery under me. The window barred and unreachable. The fast closed door.

Memories and nightmares haunted me till I hardly knew which was which. Flicker of shadow became a shaped dread of dark wings and scared wild cat eyes. . . . Falling, falling. Plunging and twisting out of the sky and the hard ground rising up.

"Mum!" . . .

I hear her move in her bed but my voice is panic-strangled and she does not wake. I gain courage to leap up and dive past the demons into her room.

"Go back to bed," she says.

"There's awful things in the kitchen, Mum. They've got wings and claws."

"Nonsense," she says. "It's the light from the stove. They're only shadows, son."

"They keep grabbing me," I whimper. "Can't I sleep with you?"

She sighs. "Keep still, then." She smoothes my hair sleepily and I relax.

No nightmares here.

She is clattering around in the kitchen when I blink awake from the tangled heap of blankets on her big double bed. Two long streams of light filter through holes in a hessian sack that covers the glassless window. There is a large battered wardrobe in a corner, a kerosene lantern on the floor, and a mirror on the wall between pictures of two people pointing at their exposed hearts. I don't know what they mean but Mum says they are holy, so I suppose they bring good luck.

Mum's always telling me how lucky we are to have

this place and her widow's pension to keep us on. She had to put up a fight to convince the authorities that she had been legally married to a white man and wanted to go on living white. Mum cried when the Welfare took the older ones away. She was soft about her kids. Then the baby died and there was only me.

She didn't take up with anyone until Mr Willy came along. He was pretty old but he was white and earned a decent enough crust from his wood-cutting. He didn't live with us, just dropped in and stayed the night sometimes. He found this place for us and got us the furniture. Mum was proud and respectable, but she wasn't a fool. If she married she would lose her pension.

"Get up out of that," she calls. "Your breakfast's been ready the last hour."

I straggle up and pull on the clothes I have left where I got out of them last night.

"Don't forget to wash," she says.

I go out to the tap, wet my hands and wipe them over my face and hair.

She ladles out a plate of steaming stew and sets it on the table in front of me.

"What is it?" I ask.

"Kangaroo tail."

"Did you get it off the old abo?"

"Stop asking questions and eat up," she says. "You're nothing but a bag of bones. They'll be saying I don't feed you next and we'll have the Welfare on to us again. You know what that'll mean."

It is a threat that always works and I get on with it.

9

"I saw that old trapper come past yesterday," I say. "Gee, he's a funny looking guy."

"You remember what I said and don't go talking to him," she says.

I'm not interested in the old blackfella but I always get a bite if I mention him.

I get up from the table and she notices my clothes.

"Looks like you've been wriggling through that drain pipe again? You haven't been with those dirty Noongar kids I hope?"

I shake my head and grin.

"It's no joking matter," she says. "If we get seen with that mob we'll be chucked out of this place quick smart."

"Some of the white kids play with them."

She starts packing up the plates. "That's different. They belong on the white side of the fence. You've got to prove you do, and don't you forget it."

Mum's always at me about this Noongar mob, though some of them seem to be related to us in a vague way. A few of them are as light coloured as herself, some even as near white as me but most of them are pretty dark skinned. None of them are real aboriginal, though sometimes a full blood relative will drift in to the camp, stay for a bit, and get on the grog with them. This kind never seems to stay long though. They just appear and disappear, except the old rabbit trapper who sticks around but lives in a camp on his own.

Most of the Noongars drift round the place too. Some of them go off on seasonal work—picking apples, digging spuds and odd jobbing at harvest and shearing time, but there are always some in this outskirt camp and when the workers come back they all get on it properly till the money runs out.

The Noongar kids are supposed to go to school, and the Welfare blokes are always chasing them up. A lot of them get shoved into missions and homes, but somehow there are always plenty who manage to dodge out—not the same ones all the time—but usually enough to have some fun with.

I bring in some wood for the fire. "There's a cricket match on in the school grounds," I say. "Can I go and watch?"

"All right. But look out you're home in good time for dinner."

I dart off and make for the stock pens across the railway line. I hear the Noongar kids shouting and laughing a long way off. They are playing follow-my-leader along the pen tops, wobbling and balancing and falling off.

"Hullo!"

"Hullo. We've been waiting ages. Thought you must be back in that old school or something."

"Nope. It's still holidays. My mum kept me yacking."

"Making you clean up that la-di-dah house, I s'pose."

Another one chips in. "That's what my mum reckons about a house. 'Not worth the bloody trouble,' she says."

The boy is bigger and darker than me and I am a bit afraid of him.

"Yes, it's pretty mad," I agree. "But Mum likes it
so we have to live in it."

"My mum reckons she's stuck up because she married a white chap and has another white man on her
now. But she weren't no better than the rest of them
before."

"She went to school and got educated," I say defensively.

"So what," he comes back. "My mum went to the
same mission only she don't get stuck in no Department house like a cocky in a cage."

Another boy says: "I wouldn't mind the house but
damn going to school. What's the good of it anyway?"

"My mum says you've got to go or you can't get
on."

"Get on where?" asks the first boy.

"Search me," I say. "Get a job I s'pose."

They look at me with dark and doubtful eyes.

"Aw, let's get moving," I say. "What're we going
to do?"

"Go after birds and rabbits. We got some gings."

This is attractive but they would probably not be
back till nearly dark and Mum would ask questions.

"What say we catch gilgies? I've got a gidgee hidden down the river bank. There's some real big ones
this time of year."

The others are not so keen on this.

"Let's go to the silos," another suggests, "and slide
down the wheat."

This is attractive too but if I'm caught with these
kids it might be all up for Mum and me. "Some kids

were copped for doing that the other day," I lie. "They got sent to clink."

"Yeah," says the big chap who is about as scared of trouble as myself. "Let's get over into the bush where no one'll bother us."

We straggle across the line and into the trees. The kids fill their pockets with little stones and trail about spotting birds and aiming without success.

"My old uncle," says the big chap, "I seen him drop birds with stones plenty times. He made a spear once too and showed me how the abos used to bring down kangaroos."

"I saw a real bush abo once could throw a boomerang," another kid says. "He had thick scars cut on his chest and arms."

"What for?" I ask.

"He reckoned they did it to all the abo boys to make them tough."

"Bet it must have hurt."

"They got trained up to it. The kids played who could keep live coals the longest in their hands or on their arms and legs and after a bit they got used to it and didn't feel the pain hardly at all."

One of the kids lends me his ging and I fool around with it a bit. A rabbit scuttles out of the grass and we all yell and get around it. I put a stone in the ging and let fly. I don't expect to hit it but it flops down and the big chap picks it up and bangs its head against a tree. The others shake my hand and hit me on the back and the big chap holds the dead rabbit out to me.

"It's yours," he says. "You knocked it down."

"No," I say, "I don't want it. We got plenty rabbits home."

I haven't seen a rabbit killed since that time in the cemetery. Mum had gone there with me and some old native woman to put flowers on my brother's grave. He was only a baby when he died and it hadn't meant much to me until this time standing beside the oblong rain-leached heap of gravel and sand. Then this rabbit bounced out of the scrub and the old woman picked up a stick and battered it. I looked down at the dead animal beside the wilting flowers in the jam jar and suddenly burst out crying and hid my face in my mum's dress. We had rabbit stew that night.

I get home late. Mum asks where I've been. I tell her just mucking about with some of the kids from school, but she knows I'm telling a lie.

"You want to stay with me, son?" she asks.

I nod and look at the floor.

"They'll take you away like the rest of them," she says.

"No!" . . .

My voice ripped out in a scream that hurled back the familiar bareness of the cell. A key mercifully grated in the lock. The door opened. The fourteen days were done.

When the warder took me back to the Juvenile Section I found I had become a hero to my mates. Even the screw became a bit human and gave me a cigarette. I was a little colder and a little older, more a part of the prison and its atmosphere, part of the grey cloud that dismally envelops it. This atmosphere got me down when I first came in but now it had become part of me. I became an emptiness gas-filled with the grey cloud.

After solitary the prison accepted me as I had never been accepted outside. I belonged.

# two

I PICK up the towel and rub myself dry but there still remains the peculiar smell of the yellow prison soap. You get used to it, but it emanates from us all, strong as vomit stink.

I follow the other soon-to-be-ex-cons into the cell-like room where our clothes await us. It is here that we were initiated into jail life and for the first time donned the grey uniform of belonging. It has the last touch of outside when we come in, the first touch when we leave. It is a sort of despair and expectation depot.

Our citizen-of-the-world clothes cringe in shadow one against the other as though anticipating the jeers in store for them. They have been tailored on a prison wage, modelled in the latest style of years gone by and made of the choicest cloth available. Blue serge that has the habit, much like its wearers, of picking up bits of fluff around the streets.

I choose a suit that looks more or less my size and put it on. The mirror reflects a person I take to be myself gazing back blank-eyed. Critically I examine the image: the figure tall and slim, the face, neither handsome nor ugly, and the skin, due to lack of sun, now no darker than olive shade. The suit is not as bad as I expected and appears to be a good fit. Either a convict is finding joy in his work or I, after eighteen months, have lost my clothes sense. Anyway, it will do until I can acquire something more suited to my taste. The people I know outside go in for clothes. They call themselves Progressive Dressers—and I have influence enough to borrow at least a shirt and a pair of jeans.

I comb my hair as best I can. It is in a crew-cut ordered by the chief warder. He must have read that bodgies wear their hair long and decided to do his bit in the fight against juvenile delinquency. Or maybe he remembered the Samson story.

I am dressed and ready to go, but we still have to wait until the screw condescends to open the door. Waiting gives me time to think about the future and toss up whether I will swing on with the gang again. I can take them or leave them now. It's amusing in a way, after being born at the bottom of the world to find I have worked myself up such a long way. I frequent the best bodgie hangouts now and sleep with white girls if I want them—great kicks. . . .

Clunkity-clunkity-bang. Clunkity-clunkity-bang. . . . Blank-faced teenagers sway to the delinquent beat, gyrate and shuffle, losing their souls to it.

> *Black, black cat where are you going to go?*
> *Black cat, so black cat when are you going to go?*

*Been sitting here all night,*
*It really ain't right,*
*You gotta go to be in the know.*

A roll of drums, and the band rests. Lights swell and show up the youth's face. False insolent face with the bleak eyes of ain't-got-nowhere-to-go.

He sweats in the stuffy hall, half suffocated by the hot reek of powdered bodies and heavily oiled hair. The mob swirls aimlessly about. One or two stop to speak to him and he answers shortly.

The band begins again. Four tight-trousered youths with gleaming electric guitars sway in anticipation of the drums and lay down a steady beat. The bass guitar clunks, the others twang and they're off.

The youth puffs on a cigarette, carefully protecting his new clothes from the ash. Smoke spirals float up and fade into the ceiling haze. The lights dim and a girl appears in front of him. Dark eyes hollow in a pale face, short ash-blonde hair. Her smeared mouth twists.

"What a drag this place is."

His eyes drop to her blouse. Small breasts. Real neat.

"What place isn't?"

She sits next to him and they watch the dancers.

"It's helluva hot, and those cats still dance."

"Mad! I saw a black cat once, it ran round and round until it dropped dead. Real crazy."

"Crazy."

She is restless and he sees that her forehead is damp.

18

"Want to get some air?"

"My date's pissed off somewhere. I guess it's all right."

They circle the floor and escape to the river bank.

She takes his hand as they stumble across the grass. Overhead the dark sky is filled with stars and a cool wind moves in the trees. They sit and he feels her body against his.

It's too much of a drag to do it now and not worth it. Sex is such a bore sometimes. All the same he feels her breast and she does not protest. It's too peaceful for anything except talk.

"Got some money yesterday and bought some new threads."

"They're terrif. I saw them in the hall. Must have cost a bit?"

"They did, but I'm a Christian and God provided me with the cash. It was a sort of debt."

"How do you mean debt?" she says.

"Church bored me crazy when I was a kid."

She seems impressed. "Hey! you didn't rob a church?"

He nods. "Donation box. It was a pushover."

He tells her how he came into the Cathedral the night before. A few people praying but no one noticing him. He slipped through a small door up the stairs. A grill barred his way to the choir gallery, so he sat down and waited until someone came to lock up the church. He went down then—pretty spooky it was. Only the sacristy lamp flickering a tiny light and shadows moving everywhere. But he had a small torch.

"I nearly knocked over St Anthony, but I begged his pardon and asked his help. He gave me the wink where I would find the box. It was there right enough and dead easy to crack. The jemmy made a bit of a noise wrenching off the lock, but nobody heard— except God, and He wasn't interested. It was a regular lucky dip—quite a few greenbacks and a pocket full of coin."

"How did you get out if it was locked up?"

"Easy. There was a door bolted from inside. I found that out to start with, see. It was a dark night and nobody could have seen me leave."

"You're game," she says. "You must have needed the money pretty bad to dare God."

*Ain't no God no more, no more.*
*There ain't no God no more. Yeah!*

His fingers unfasten her blouse and dip inside her bra. She laughs. Her hand moves. . . .

It isn't worth it. Got a willing chick here and can't be bothered doing anything. Not tonight.

They end on the ground kissing for a time, then he sits up and talks again.

"Listen. You know what? I want to go over to the East and become something. I'm washed up here— done. Done everything I can do. If I go fruit-picking or work on a farm I can save enough money to go across."

"Why don't you? I wish I could go, but my mother takes most of my money off me."

Silence. For something to do he snaps the strap of her bra. This brings a giggle. He watches the reflec-

tions of the city lights broken by the ripples. The
river smells like blood. Swellings and hollows. He
moves his hands away in disgust.

"Let's go get a cup of coffee."

"What about my date?"

"Oh forget about him. He can find his own way
home."

"Yeah. I'm thirsty. When I go out with him he
never buys me a drink or anything."

"O.K., O.K."

They tidy their clothes.

Expresso bar softly lighted. They take a corner
table and drink black coffee. He yawns, she yawns.
They wander back to the hall where her date takes
her off his hands. The dance is about over and he drifts
off.

*Black, black cat where are you going to go? . . .*

I should be happy I'm getting out, but I'm not. At
this moment going out is meaningless. What exactly
am I going out for? God knows. In here I can achieve
a certain evenness of mind, but out there it will go
like my prison suit.

I glance at the bleak greyness of the walls. Even
in the quivering sunlight they retain their clamminess,
recalling the nightmares that chilled my prison sleep
and vaguely haunted my daylight hours.

The walls are rough sandstone blocks with shrunken
lime between. High and thick they loom around, and
on top at vantage points sit the flimsy glass and corrugated iron guard boxes. I look up and see the guard,
death stick at the ready, peering down at us. Grey for

walls, yellow for boxes, blue for guards, static and distinct.

Outside they may think these screws are ordinary men doing a job for the community, but to us they are a pack of wage slaves with a taste for brutality. Who makes a job for them anyway? Without us cons they would be nothing.

We move across to the superintendent's office to collect our miserable prison pay. I throw my chest out and march, really step out to show my acquaintances that I am on my way. Yesterday I had to listen to their stale jokes, like "See you in a week", and so. on. Not really funny because it might so easily be true.

We stand in front of the grey main building, a line of clowns with haphazard smiles revealing our uncertainty. Should we feel happy? Sad? Or in between? We are the I-don't-care-a-damn-mob. We fake it when we can't make it.

This chap Jeff in front of me turns and talks out of the side of his mouth.

"I know this doll with the big tits. And man, can she turn it on!"

Jeff and I once shared the misery of a boys' home when we were kids and we swung together for a while in jail. Not really friends, only acquaintances for time-killing talks on Sunday afternoons. God and eternity, being and non-being etc. We couldn't agree on any answers, but it gave me a chance to air my highbrow reading. It wasn't altogether a waste of time because he really knows a lot. He is a sincere Catholic —one of those cons who get intensely religious in jail, and he tried to bring me back to the One True Faith. Once he softened me up enough to go to Mass with him, but it only brought me back to the awful boredom of the orphanage.

In my mind's eye the school chapel looms up, cream-walled with stained glass windows, the tower pointing at a star, the boys filing in for prayers. Inside, all subdued brown—highly polished floors, rafters, pews, pulpit and altar rails, and around the dome of the sanctuary a fresco of the hung Christ. The principal mounting the pulpit, his face intense and old, his lips pursed to speak:

"How can there be secrets unknown to the living God? He is everywhere and He sees into the hearts of each and every one of you. He sees into the deepest and blackest cave. He is awake to all your lies and all your tricks. I tell you God is not mocked. No! And those boys who stole oranges from the orchard last Saturday. Yes, you were seen. You refused to step forward and confess—but God is not blind. He can blast you down at this very moment and send your souls straight to the everlasting fires of Hell. Boys, boys look into your hearts. Let each and every one of you dredge up the hidden slime and cast the devil away from you. Make a deep examination of your consciences and a sincere act of contrition, resolving to sin no more. . . ."

Jeff went to Mass as regularly in jail as he did in school and prayed for salvation. He wasn't faking then. But what a change now that he's coming out!

"You'll have something worth confessing if you go with that hot-stuff doll again."

He grins and looks embarrassed.

It is time to move. The screw orders us to file into the Administration Section. This department is a sort of brain, an invisible place from which orders flash along telephone wires. We never go there except on our day of release. The trusties do not look like convicts at all. They are clerk-like and efficient in well-made prison drab, a contrast to the rest of us, always sloppy and soiled. It is obvious that they take pains to groom themselves, like white-collar suckers who want to catch the boss's eye. Here they keep tidy to keep their cushy jobs.

For myself I don't care a damn how I dress in jail. The only time I became enthusiastic was when a shipment of ex-army trousers came in. Man, they were really bodgie pants. We each got a pair and an over-sized coat, and strutted about being all jazz-like and calling each other "man" or "Dad". Real delinquents, just like the movies. The day the chief warder noticed us we had drifted way out from the norm and were going round with the bottoms rolled half way up our calves. Joke over! Back to the old drabs.

The superintendent walks out of his office holding our money in little envelopes. Our earnings are small enough, but we have not worked too hard for them, and what we did helped to fill in the long, drifting weeks and days.

The superintendent is getting on in years and so is his brown suit. He looks the personification of the prison and radiates the same dreariness. He is one of us even though he considers himself free. Perhaps once this man felt he could reform convicts, lead them on to the straight and narrow, but I see now that in his way he is as lost as the rest of us. Maybe even more. He had more to lose.

He hands us the money and wearily begins his fare-well and don't-do-it-again speech, which means, "See you tomorrow mate." His voice grinds out the dirge that mocks us, mocks him and mocks the world.

It's over and we're on our way. We file out to-gether and I alone look back. I want to pound on the locked gates and demand to be let in again. . . . I turn away. So long jail for now—or for ever?

# II
# FREEDOM

# three

OUTSIDE at last and what to do? Got to get a move on or be picked up for loitering with intent. Lucky others, vanished into the streets below to somewhere or someone. But how would you come back from jail to a wife and family? Try to be cheerful? "Hullo I'm back. How're you all going?" Words running out into a silence. . . . Wife tongue-tied. There can be no questions about jail. Tears have dried up long ago —if there were any. Probably there is a boy-friend now and nothing to be said except Hullo—Good-bye. Then off somewhere to get drunk. Big deal.

I am still in front of the gates, staring down the hill and over the port. It is summer and the sun is white-hot metal in the sky. The rippling sea glints back and cheers me. Good rocking tonight.

The people in their light summer clothes make moving patterns against the drab stone buildings. I drag myself slowly downhill into the problem-filled future, and already I begin to feel homesick for the easy drifting of boob. I guess the fact is I'm afraid of life, haven't got the guts to be a real criminal.

The sea is near and I walk to it, remembering nights in jail when its singing blackness was distant and unattainable. My cell was on the top landing and in winter when the sea-wind came crying in I stood on the bed, face pressed to the bars, gulping the salt sea tang until I became part of its crashing surf and soundless depths. Brain-washed, body-washed, drifting in a trance. . . . On clear nights I could see the water alight under the space-travelling moon and I would feel detached from life, melancholy but content.

"Hey you! Get down from that window." The harsh frog voice of the warder would fling me back into my cell. It was against regulations to forget my punishment among the stars. Convicts standing at windows could be contemplating escape—although the ground was floodlit and forty feet below.

The hill ends, and the shops flaunting their wares solicit me like harlots. I walk into a store and stand gaping idiotically at the brightly stacked shelves. Mouth waters at the rows of tins, jars and boxes of luxury foods, but habit checks my greed. I was raised in poverty; it has disciplined by appetite, and anything that fills my belly is good enough.

"Yes?"

The old lady behind the counter is a picture of church-going respectability. I feel her pious horror as she glances at my unmistakable prison suit. I pretend not to notice her, but from the corner of one eye observe an agitated blue-veined hand. What is she frightened of? The old duck's past raping age and her shop is too near the jail to be raided by a con.

"Packet of cigarettes, please. Any sort will do."

She takes a packet from the shelf.

"No, not those. The blue ones over there."

"That'll be three and three."

She watches my every movement as I pull out my pay packet, open it and hand her a ten bob note. She rings it into the till, puts my change on the counter and watches nervously. I act my crim role again, pick up the change coin by coin and slowly take out and light a cigarette, giving her time to imagine all sorts of possibilities before I step out into the street.

Cars zoom past. Laden trucks lumber and clatter to and from the wharf. Fremantle is a busy port buzzing with movement, everyone but me with somewhere to go. While I was inside some zealous prison worker asked me if I knew where I was going. I said a ticket was put into my hand when I was born, but if it gave a destination, well, time had smudged the ink and so far no collector had come to clear the matter up.

No one spares a glance for the half-breed delinquent, and this is how I want it. I steer away from the ships and turn towards the beach. A few people splash in the mild surf or lie about exposing pink limbs to the burning sun. Funny how they oil themselves over and bake to achieve the despised colour I was born with. Some kids are building a castle in the white wet sand, flat-topped with bucket-shaped turrets and a moat. It is the same sort they all build, so maybe it is the kind of place white people dream of living in— pretentious, dominating and secure.

I never had clean beach sand to play on when I was a kid. In fact never saw the sea before I was nine, so

I used to build things out of mud. I can see myself now squatting in a corner of the big paddock, small and thin and brown in my patched khaki pants and shirt, lost in the creation of a remembered town. I always built this same place, shaping walls of mud, doors and roofs of bark, and all around among untidy lumps of mud I made tower things from sticks above holes in the ground. In my mind's eye the houses were all painted dazzling white, and the big hotel on the corner was red brick with a cast iron balcony and corrugated iron roof. The other things were mines and slag heaps and poppet heads, and stretching away from them I would see the spare desert scrub shimmering to a flat horizon and the whole land panting with heat under a bleached blue sky.

When the other kids found me they used to laugh and break up my mining town. Then I began building towns full of white goblins and I stamped them into the ground in a rage.

A kid comes yelling along the beach and loudly displays a cut foot to his fussing mum. She carts him to the water, washes off the sand and takes a tin of sticking plaster from the pocket of her beach gown. The kid stops yelling and runs off and I stretch myself out on the sand remembering that day I cut my own foot on a jagged piece of glass. I yelled too and my mum got a handful of cobwebs from a corner of the house and put them over the gash. She had some idea about cobwebs. I don't know. Anyway the cut stopped bleeding and she tied it up but I went on snivelling to hold her sympathy.

"You've got to learn to be a man," she said. "It's

a tough world and there'll come a time you won't have a mum to come crying to."

I shut up then and I felt a sort of shiver of dread like always when I thought of being taken away from her. That was the day Mr Willy took me out with him. A good day. I lie on my back, one arm across my eyes and remember it. . . .

A slow-moving cloud of dust shapes itself into a horse and cart. Now it is close enough for me to make out the red face, white hair and fierce moustache of Mr Willy. He is over seventy but he jumps off the cart like a young fellow.

"Hullo, Mr Willy. You taking me along with you today?"

"Yes, kid, today's the day."

Mum is watching from the doorway, her long black hair hanging in two plaits almost to her waist. Her face is shining with pleasure and she is so beautiful I feel a lump in my throat.

"You're taking him?" she calls. "Sure he won't be a nuisance? Come in a minute and I'll get you some bread and jam to take along."

"Mind the horse," he says, "while I have a word with your mum."

It is a long word. I watch the horse as its big mouth feels around for the grass and its yellow teeth munch steadily and the heat of the summer day beats down. At last Mr Willy comes out alone. He has a satisfied look and a parcel of lunch wrapped in newspaper.

"Come on, son. Hop up."

I swing myself into the cart, my legs dangling over the back.

With a "Gidiap" and a lurch we move off at last and when the horse breaks into a trot I have a job to keep from sliding backwards. I don't mind this though, I'm just so pleased when Mr Willy takes me out. A nosebag full of chaff, a waterbag and two axes in leather holders bounce around in the back with me. We go real fast. The cloppetty hoofs and the rattly wheels make a kind of song.

We turn off down a rough side track with trees and shrubs pushing in on either side. About a mile along Mr Willy stops the cart, gets down and hangs his coat over a branch. He unharnesses the horse, puts on its nosebag, and gets the axes out.

"You can go off and play, son. Not too far though. I'll give you a holler at dinner time."

"Can I climb the hill?" I ask.

"You can try," he laughs. "Be careful though, it's pretty steep."

I feel grown up. He would never let me try before. I scramble through prickly scrub and between huge boulders. The hill rises sharply now and my eyes measure the distance to the top. I grasp at branches and hang like a monkey, searching for footholds. It is a real hard climb for a kid and I am panting when I get to the top. I fling myself down, my chest heaving, my hands and legs scratched and stinging. A warm wind soon dries up the sweat. I get up and look into the valley, away, away down. The big boulders seem like pebbles from here and the trees like shrubs. The horse looks no bigger than a dog, the cart like a

34

toy and Mr Willy like a sort of insect as he swings his axe. I am king of the castle on the highest mountain in the world.

Sunlight glints from the axe head and its sound echoes against the hill. A tree comes slowly, slowly down, rises as if trying to struggle up again and then hits the ground with a final thud. The Willy insect clambers over the branches and begins to lop them off.

Hilltop eyes do a circuit of the countryside. A haze of smoke marks the position of the town but I don't like this town and look the other way. A kangaroo bounds out of the scrub around the foothills, then a man appears carrying something in his hands. I screw up my eyes against the glare and I see it is the old blackfellow who sometimes calls on my mum and gives her rabbits or kangaroo. The things in his hands must be his rabbit traps. He has never really talked to me. Just smiled and said "Good day" and walked quietly away, so I don't know his name. He doesn't look scarey, but some of the Noongar kids say he is a magic man and is as old as the sky, and that they have seen him talking to snakes and kangaroos.

I hear a cooee and look down the other side of the hill. The insect man is shading his eyes with his hand trying to spot me up here on my mountain top.

Oh well, the king must go down now and have some bread and jam. He is hungry anyway.

A cascade of rocks and gravel slide down with me. I leave a path of destruction and rip the seat out of my pants.

The billy is boiling when I get back to the cart. Mr Willy flings in the tea leaves and pours the steaming brew into my battered enamel pannikin. I pile it up with sugar and sip cautiously between large bites of bread.

"Get a good view from up there?" Mr Willy asks.

"The whole world," I say.

"Hmm," says Mr Willy and shakes his white head. "The world's a big place, son."

"I know," I say. And I feel it is a good and wonderful world.

The sun is midway down the sky and the trees are all cut into suitable lengths for loading. I help Mr Willy stack the cart and harness the horse between the shafts again. I get on the top of the load, Mr Willy sits up in front and the cart sways out on to the track again.

"Had a good day, son?" Mum asks.

"Yeah, it was mighty," I say. "I climbed to the top of the big hill and who do you think I saw?"

"How should I know?" she asks.

"The funny old black man with the rabbit traps."

"You didn't go near him I hope? You didn't talk to him?"

"Why not?" I ask. "What's the matter with him?"

"He's a bit mad," she says. "I said you were never to talk to him."

I can't kid her any longer. "Arrr, Mum. I was right on top of the hill and he was down near the bottom. He didn't even see me." . . .

"Mummy, Mummy. Come and look at our castle. Isn't it beaut?"

36

A woman looks up from her magazine with bored eyes. "It's lovely darling."

I sit up and she smiles across at me as though we two grown-ups share a secret about childish fantasies. I suppose she expects me to smile back, but I scowl. She suddenly sees me as a stranger and stares coldly at the darkness of my skin. I run my eyes over her legs, her hips and her breasts. She glances down, assures herself that there is nothing showing and looks distastefully into my sullen face. So what? If she rejects me, I rejected her first.

I drift away past the little groups, looking for a place to myself.

# four

SOMEONE else has thought of the same thing. She lies
stretched out in the sun and her skin is golden-brown.
Swell doll. Long and slim with firm small breasts
tightening the fabric of her white swim suit. I realize
that jail has not killed my sex urge.

I can't tell whether she has noticed me behind her
big sun glasses, so I light a cigarette and think of
something to say to make the scene. The sea supplies
the mood music, a cool noise with a throbbing base
melody. I fling away the cigarette and flop down, at
a loss for an opening. She does not stir. I watch her
and fake that she is a princess wrecked on some bar-
baric shore and I am the hero about to rescue her.
How corny can you get? She's only a half-naked
chick asleep on the beach within an hour's walk of
the jail.

I take off my shoes, socks, coat, ludicrous tie and
cheap shirt and stretch out a few feet away. It gets
boring after a while.

I say, "Hullo!"

No reply.

"Like are you dead, or only in a Yogi trance?"

She moves.

I say the "Hullo" word again and she lifts her head to peer at me behind the disguise of her dark glasses. Then she raises herself on her elbow. My appearance must be registering. She could be the sort of person who finds me interesting. Sometimes they do, but the majority wouldn't help me up if I fainted. If she doesn't like the look of me she can move off, but why can't she say something? The silence is getting on my nerves. Only sometimes I get this feeling I want to talk and make someone understand the way I think. Of course people never do. Mostly they cut me off after the first few don't-care words and start handing out stupid advice and I just freeze up inside. Still, I have this tiny hope that some day someone will listen and nearly understand.

She says "Hullo," but she sounds like cold.

I say, "It's a nice day for the beach." Standard clichés are all right for a start.

"Wonderful," she says.

She sounds educated and I have to let her know her type doesn't impress me.

"Wonderful to have time to loaf, isn't it?" I say. "Not a care in the world."

"Haven't you?" she asks. "Good for you."

"Not so good," I say. "I'm one of the permanent unemployed unemployables. No rich family to bludge on either."

"Too bad," she says, glances at her wrist watch and begins to flick the sand from her legs with a towel.

I can see she's going to get up and go away. "Sorry

for being such a drag," I say. "Just felt I'd rather like to talk to someone besides myself for a change."

She stops flicking the towel and gives a kind of half smile.

"I know. Get bored with myself sometimes too."

I feel suddenly annoyed. As if a girl like her could understand about the way I feel.

"You don't know anything. You haven't just got out of bloody jail."

If she's going away, I might as well make my mark with her. I wait for the look of shocked surprise, but for all she registers I might as well have told her I'd just come off an innocent little river trip.

"So now you'll be able to run home and tell them you've met a real live jailbird."

"That'll rock them for sure," she says and stifles a small yawn. "How long were you in?"

"Eighteen months, this time. Breaking and entering."

She takes it dead pan.

"Sounds as though you're used to it anyway. How long until next time?"

I shrug. "Who cares?"

"Can't be so bad if that's the way it is," she says.

"It kills the time."

"What do you do in there?" she asks. "Besides crack stones and skite about your jobs?"

"Aw . . . eat, sleep, swap dirty yarns, read paperbacks, cut pictures of naked women out of magazines. They're supposed to arouse desire."

"And do they?"

"Usually. It was only a drag though."

40

"That all you did?"

"I had to sweep out the library and used to smuggle books out of there. Real highbrow stuff—classics, psychology. And semi-religious books for intellectual sterilization. They had the best stuff under key in the staff section but I managed to pick the lock. Got a bloke to smuggle me in a little kerosene lamp and rigged my blankets so the screw couldn't see the light. Read nearly all night."

"What did you make of the psychology?"

"Plenty. Learnt I'm a manic depressive, neurotic, psychotic, schizophrenic—the works."

She seems interested. I've hooked her.

"How much education did you have?" she asks.

"I went to an ordinary school for a couple of years," I tell her. "There I learnt the art of survival against mob rule. Then I got copped for stealing and I was sent to a home where I was educated in the simple techniques of crime and learnt to survive the harshness of Christian charity. In the Noongar camps I learnt the art of being completely unexploitable and of sabotaging every make-believe effort to improve the native's lot. I also learnt to take raw alcohol and raw sex. In jail I graduated in vice and overcame my last illusions about life. Now I know that hope and despair are equally absurd."

"Is there anything left?" she asks.

I shrug. "Excuses I suppose. I still have enough intelligence to make excuses for myself. I can say that the prison warped my mind, that when I first went in I still had some vestige of childish faith. Or I can put it down to my colour, being born under the curse of Ham and all that jazz."

She seems to be looking at me more closely than before.

"Maybe you couldn't see I was coloured through those things you wear."

"You don't show it much, except in the way you move. More supple than a white boy. I might have taken you for Mexican, maybe. Or Southern European."

"My mum was half-caste," I tell her, "but my dad was white. He was a prospector. I was born on the goldfields. Don't remember it much except it was good there. After he died mum came to the wheat-belt. She thought we'd have more chance there, but it didn't make any difference."

A brawny surf-lifesaver type passes along the sea front and her eyes follow him. The bitch isn't listening to me, not that I expect her to be interested.

"Well, where do you go from here?" she asks suddenly. "I mean—I suppose you've got to do something between this and your next time in."

"Sure," I say. "Get drunk, feed a few juke boxes, have a few girls till my prison pay runs out."

"Then what?"

"I'll be lucky to be out that long."

"You mean you've planned to do a job straight away?"

"I never plan ahead. I just wait for life to happen to me."

"But they can't put you in until you deliberately break the law."

42

"You haven't got a clue," I tell her. "They make the law so chaps like me can't help breaking it whatever we do, and the likes of you can hardly break it if you try."

"How do you mean?" she asks.

"For one thing. We make the only friends we have in jail, but if we're seen talking outside we're arrested for consorting with crims."

"What's to stop you getting an ordinary job?"

"Plenty," I say. "The complete absurdity of it for a start—tearing your guts out in some mechanized rat cage. No thanks."

"So you've never tried to get a job?"

"Sure I did, but I wasn't in the race. Who wants a shiftless native when he can get a big up and coming Dago to work for him? After a few tries I resigned myself. Prison was the only chance I had of three meals a day and a decent bed."

"You know," she says, "the trouble with you is you've got intelligence but no guts."

This gets under my skin. "You reckon it didn't take guts to get where I am?"

"Does it take guts to get copped so you can bludge on the taxpayer?"

"I never tried to get copped," I say, "not yet, that is. I suppose you don't reckon it took guts to pinch a car and leave it outside a police station?"

She laughs. "You can call it guts if you like."

"I got clean away with that and a few other things and I worked my way right up with the gang."

"I get the picture," she says. "From outcast native to big time bodgie. Success story."

"Sure."

"And having climbed the social ladder to this dizzy height what now?"

"Who cares?" Which is what I always say when questions begin to bore me.

"The gang maybe. I expect they'll be glad to see you back."

I shrug. "It was swell being in with them until I made it to the top. They looked up to me then because they had no brains and no ideas and now I'm bored to hell with them."

"Well, if you've got any guts you'll give them away and start again."

"I'm too old now," I say.

"How old?" she asks.

"Nineteen."

"Practically Methuselah."

"Too old to laugh or cry any more. So old my bones ache."

"That's inactivity," she says. "Look here, you want to get yourself a pair of bathing trunks, get into the sea, run along the sand, lie in the sun."

"And then," I say, "something new will happen for me? A volcano of fresh hope will erupt for me?"

"That's up to you," she says.

I feel the old bitter taste of resentment in my mouth. Nothing ever up to *them*. Only up to us, the outcast relics in the outskirt camps. The lazy, ungrateful rubbish people, who refuse to co-operate or integrate or even play it up for the tourist trade. Flyblown descendants of the dispossessed erupting their hopelessness in petty crime. I glare at her with con-

centrated hate. I want to wither her glib white arro-
gance with biting scorn, but I can't find the words.

"Well you should know," I say. "I suppose there's
plenty times you've been cold and hungry and afraid.
So I'll take your advice and join the Lifesavers. Maybe they'll teach me to swim so I can save myself."

She glances at her watch.

"I'm sorry," she says, "but my time's about up. I've
an appointment in half an hour."

"Important engagement with a golf ball I suppose."

"Not golf," she says. "I'm a poor slogging student
at the University."

"What do you study?" I ask.

"Psychology, as a matter of fact."

"You'll go far," I say. "Every post a winning post,
even a neurotic jailbird on the beach."

"Look here," she protests, good-humouredly, "who
forced this conversation, anyway?"

"I should have smelt the profit motive when you
didn't knock me back. Well, you've about squeezed
the lemon dry now, so that's it."

"Have it your own way," she says. "But there's
enough juice left in the lemon yet to keep the profit
motive interested."

"You're kidding," I say.

"Call my bluff then," she says. "Meet me at the
Uni coffee lounge tomorrow afternoon and meet
some of my gang. It'll be a change for you, anyway."

I stand up and watch her as she pulls on a sweater
and skirt. She names a time and tells me how to find
my way. I want to tell her to go to hell but somehow
all the fight drains out of me. She has a swell body, a

nice voice and what I can see of her face is all right too. She is a change from the ignorant giggling chicks I have known before and it might be worth seeing her again. Typical boy meets girl on beach.

The sun sprays blood as it drops into the sea. "Well, I'll be seeing you," she says. She takes off her glasses and her eyes are wide and blue. She is about the prettiest doll I have ever seen, but she is as far away from me as the wide blue sky.

# five

THE girl has gone and I must move on again.

I make my way to the railway station, buy a ticket to Perth and drift about the platform like one of the stray sheets of newspaper waiting for a wind to blow it away. The lines hum and the train rickracks to a stop. I get in, find a place and lean back, propping my feet on the opposite seat. I notice there's a railway law against this (Regulation 166B), but I stay as I am.

A middle-aged couple enter at the first stop and look in disgust at my sprawling legs and my cigarette in a non-smoking compartment. They seat themselves as far away as possible and we ignore each other until the city lights jerk into view. The train pulls to a stop and I walk out alone into a roar of traffic and a dazzle of neon signs.

I wander down the main street, alone in the crowd. It is against the law to sleep out in the city, so I must find a room. I turn into an alley swaying with shadows and knock at a place advertising rooms to let. An old woman shows me up a flight of stairs into a small room where a weak ceiling globe reveals a bed,

47

cupboard, table and chair. I take it and pay a week's rent in advance and she gives me the key.

I sit on the sagging bed and work out my next move; brood about friends for a time and find that friendship has no meaning for me. It is only a word, but I do have acquaintances and one of these will lend me clothes. I will go and see him now.

Out in the street again, I dawdle past a music shop from which comes the sound of a familiar song . . . *Trouble in mind. I'm blue.* . . . A solitary drummer beats a slow death beat behind the words. A single saxophone wails out in long drawn notes of pain. Blue shades of the sorrowing dark people, all with trouble in mind. . . . The voice of an old-young negress singing into my heart . . . *Trouble in mind.*

Always trouble in mind. "Don't make trouble, son," Mum had said when I told her how the white kids laughed at me and kicked my case along the road. She hoped I'd make friends with them but I never did. They played with me at school when they had to, but outside the school gates they only picked on me. I didn't tell her at first until she got wild about the case and my torn shirts. One day I found her mending them and saw that she was crying. So I told her it was O.K. and I didn't care. "They're only jealous because I get top marks," I told her. "And when I'm grown up I'm going to be rich and buy you pretty dresses like the white kids' mums've got." She laughed and rumpled my hair and told me to grow up quick so she'd still be pretty enough for them. . . .

At the corner of the main street I pause for breath

outside a cellar grating and stoop to peer inside. It's the storeroom of a shop, full of packing cases and parcels and long rolls of linoleum and material.

I grasp one of the bars with my free hand and notice that the grating is loose and the thought comes into my head that I could probably squeeze in at the side. There would be all sorts of wonderful things in there—things we looked at in shop windows but could never buy, like the dresses, and the sheets Mum is always talking about. Some day, she keeps saying, she'll have sheets for her bed. And I can see dresses too, pretty shop-made ones. Mum makes her own clothes as well as mine out of cheap material, but she would look real good in a shop-made dress.

I can see stairs from the cellar that go up into the shop. There would be money in there. I could go to the movies, buy heaps of comics and tell Mum I'd picked them up on the road. If I got a dress and some sheets I could tell her I had found them in a box that fell off a carrier's truck. Things did fall off trucks and she'd believe that. . . .

Saturday night. I lie awake in my bed waiting for the town to go to sleep. The pub should close at nine o'clock, but being Saturday it stays open illegally unless there's a mean cop in the town. I know when it closes because Mr Willy will come out then. Saturday is always a gay night for him and he stays to the end. At last I hear him come stumbling towards the house.

"Good night," he calls out.

That means he isn't coming in. Too tired and drunk, I suppose, and rolling home to his own bed. His boots sound away.

49

I let time stream by for a while before I get up. The kitchen fire is dead and the street lights turned off. Mum is at last asleep and my bare feet make no noise as I slide out the door. There is no one about. I am scared but the thought of Mum's face when she sees the things I've got for her makes me brave.

I was right about the grating. I can get through quite easily. . . .

The big town cop shrinks the kitchen as he comes in the door. I look at Mum. Her eyes are scared and defiant. The cop grudgingly removes his cap, lifts an eyebrow as he looks about and clears his throat.

"I've come about the boy."

"He's done nothing. He's a good boy."

"There's been a breaking and entering job in town, and I've reason to suspect your son is the culprit."

"It can't be him. He's never pinched anything. Never done anything wrong. You've picked on him because he's coloured, that's all."

The cop shrugs. "I have a warrant and I intend to search this place."

"Go ahead," she says. "You won't find anything. He's not a thief."

I stand in the corner, shaking with fear. The cop pokes around the house and looks under my bed where I'd put the money and the comics. I had given her the dress and a pair of sheets, but I was still working out the story for the other things.

"I'm taking these things as evidence," the cop says. "I'll be back here soon."

I look at my mum and see that her expression is no

longer defiant. It is sort of beaten and servile.

He clumps out the door. Mum crumples like she has been hit in the stomach. After a while she comes over to me and we cling together. I cry because I am scared. She cries because she knows I will be taken away from her.

In the afternoon the copper returns to hand us a summons.

"On Thursday at ten o'clock you will bring the boy along to the courthouse. Ten o'clock. Understand?"

"Yes."

The sky is overcast as we make our way along the gravel road and turn the corner into the town. It is as quiet as any week day in a small country place. No one notices a coloured woman and a boy. Nobody knows. We are a bit early as Mum does not want it held against us that we are late. She stops and looks in a shop window. On one side there is a flash bedroom suite and on the other dresses on hangers, all pulled in at the waist and the bargain prices marked. She looks up and sees it is the shop I have robbed and she hurries on.

The police officer is waiting in nervous expectation. The hands of the clock are just on ten and he probably thinks his birds have gone bush. His face relaxes as we come in and he shepherds us to our places. I cling close to Mum and we both wait for the worst. Up to now she has always protected me but I know that this is something out of her control. There are just the two of us against the world.

I look across at the long table and the white men

around it who have come to decide my fate. I look down at the dusty floor and the long, dirt-caked cracks between the boards. I look up at the slime yellow walls seeking a spot on which to concentrate. My eyes rest on an enlarged photograph of the reigning monarch. Defender of the Faith. Whatever that means. The royal eyes look down coldly and accusingly. No hope there. I look away, quickly scanning the large stern men on their large pompous bottoms. They stare vacantly at the table top as the constable reads his statement.

During the night of Saturday the first of April the premises of Mr Cox of this town had been broken and entered. On examining the grating abutting on the street he found that it had been forced to provide entry. From the restriction of the entrance, he decided that a child or children were responsible and, acting on his suspicions, he had questioned various residents of the town and finally the mother of the defendant. On conducting a search of her house he had found the stolen goods. From what can be ascertained the mother knew nothing of the crime and in no way encouraged her son.

"Thanks constable. That's quite enough. Will the defendant please stand."

The Magistrate beckons and I stumble to my feet and stand alone.

"Answer the following questions truthfully. Did you or did you not break into Mr Cox's shop?"

"I did, sir."

"How did you force entry, that is get into the place?"

"I found the grating was loose accidentally, sir. I was just mucking about and found I could get in."

"Was anyone with you?"

"No, sir. I was all by myself. Only me it was, sir." My voice breaks into a whimper.

"Good. You can sit down."

My mother is now told to stand.

"Did you know what your boy was up to?"

"No, sir. He used to bring home things from the dump, some of it real good stuff too. Then he said he picked up this parcel off the road. That's the God's honest truth, sir. If I'd known he was stealing it I would have stopped him, sir, but he's always been a good boy, sir. I didn't think——"

"Yes, yes. I believe you knew nothing about it. You can take the boy home now. The constable will call on you later."

The last day of freedom. Mum and I are standing beside the policeman on the station platform and I am crying as the clock ticks the minutes away. At last the train comes in.

"Never mind, son. Everything will come out all right."

I sob and cling to her. Nothing will ever be all right now. I have been tried and found guilty. And I am already nine years old. . . .

"Trouble in mind. . . ." To hell with sentimental memories! I've been through a helluva lot of trouble in the ten years since that snivelling kid left his mum and his home town for the Boys' Home near the city. Boys' Home . . . bloody awful joke that was. And it was the end of any sort of home for me. The end of Mum too by the look of her last time I was outside. Couldn't get away from her fast enough with her whining about her ailments and how none of her kids ever came to see her now. As if I didn't have enough to do looking after myself. And right now that means getting out of this blue serge prison suit.

I reach the house where my acquaintance lives. His mother answers the door and when I tell her who I am she says to wait. He comes to the door and asks me in. He seems surprised to see me and is nervous though he fakes pleased. He flings questions at me and I answer him. He bores me and as soon as possible I put it on him for the clothes. He did a job with me once. I took the rap for us both, but he knows I could still put him in if I liked. He takes me to his room where I choose black jeans, black shirt, black desert boots. I ask him to look after the prison rig for me and he says O.K. I can collect them any time I like. He offers me a drink and we have a few whiskies. Then I glide like a black shadow into the street.

The night is still young, so I turn towards the milkbar where the old gang hangs out.

# six

I LOOK through the window of the lighted milk-bar
and the familiar surroundings glow a "Welcome
Home" to me. This joint is the meeting place of the
bodgie-widgie mob. Here they all are—the anti-socials,
the misfits, the delinks, in a common defiance of the
squares. The juke-box, a mass of metal, lights and
glass, commands the room, squat god worshipped and
fed by footloose youth to fill their empty world with
the drug-delusion of romance. It flashes me a sarcastic
grin and blares a Rock 'n' Roll hullo. I'm back and
the gang crowds round—the boys in peacock-gaudy
long coats and narrow pants, the girls casual in
dowdy-dark jeans and sloppy sweaters.

They question me about jail—who's in and who's
getting out soon? As one of the mob I have to answer
them. Then they tell me about their own activities,
the last week-end party and the latest dance hall that
chucked them out. One chap has been picked up for
carnal knowledge, another for car stealing. I sympa-
thize and bum a cigarette and laugh at the funny bits.

Already I'm bored and feel depressed from the whisky I've had.

I drift away to a vacant table, order sandwiches and cigarettes and whisper for a cup of wine. The waiter says he is glad to see me back and passes me a bottle with a reminder about the cops. I fill my cup and put the bottle under the table. The music comes out good and sad. . . .

> *You can get rid of loneliness*
> *If you can fall in love. . . .*

A theme song for the kids.

I sit and drink, peering through the haze of smoke.

"Hi, man!"

Big hazel eyes stare down at me. Long lashes flicker.

"I'm drunk, doll."

"Like I can see that."

"Sure am."

I look at her as she hums a few bars of the song. It is that moment of drink when the fog rolls back and the mind clears. Every object becomes detached, vivid, intense and stark. Nothing runs into anything else. This girl Denise stands there transfixed in time.

Big eyes glow, lips nature-red are parted revealing strong slightly stained teeth. Dark hair is alive, writhing to her shoulders to frame the moon-pale oval of her face. She still attracts me. Denise is one of the few people with whom I never have to pose.

She is a semi-pro. I met her at a dance one night a couple of years ago. I paid her the first time but not after that. I couldn't care less what she does. Making money that way is better than working and her family feels the same. She lives at home, but all they worry about is the rent money.

We are glad to find each other here again. I talk.

"How're you going?"

"O.K. Thought of joining the Salvation Army to see you inside."

"You'd have made a real hep hymn singer."

She sits down next to me.

"I've got a bottle of wine under the table," I say.

"Wasting your prison dough."

"Why not?"

"Yeah. That's right. Why not?"

She walks to the counter to get a cup.

"It's vile stuff," she says, tasting the grog. "No wonder you look rotten."

"I'm miserable."

"I've got some pills that'll sober you up and give you a lift. Take a couple and then we can get pissed together."

She takes a small bottle from her pocket and gives me two yellow tablets. I gulp them down with a cup of wine. A mistake. The clearness fogs and the world grows dull again, but the music still shrieks sharply through my head. I feel bad now, real bad. Sick drunk fool! Crazy, I'm way down in the blues. Got a ten ton load on my head. I get up and fall back on to my chair. Rest on her shoulder.

"You're really drunk now, ain't you, mate?" Her voice is low-pitched and soothing.

"I know."

"The pills will hit you in a minute. They're great kicks."

She walks to the juke-box and back with a hip wriggle that makes me think of bed.

"I've picked a couple of good numbers that'll cheer you up."

She's kidding me. The sad tune makes me ache with loneliness.

> *The bell-hop's tears keep flowing,*
> *The desk clerk's dressed in black.*
> *They've been so long down lonely street*
> *That they'll never, oh never, come back.*
> *'Cause they're so lonely, oh so lonely,*
> *They're so lonely they could die.*

The voice wails out to reach me, but now the pills are taking effect and I can contemplate my mood objectively.

Denise goes on drinking to get drunk. I go on to stay that way. The juke-box keeps playing. Mind flows with the rhythm and follows the sad-sounding horn. I put my arm around Denise and fake togetherness.

It's late and the waiter hovers about wanting to close the joint. I buy another bottle of wine and we stagger out. The coolness of early morning sobers me a bit and I'm feeling sick by the time we reach my room.

I switch on the light and open the bottle of wine. Denise puts down her little transistor radio and switches to an all-night station. I have a swig, go to the bathroom, put my head under the tap and dry it on someone else's towel. Come back to the room tired but not sleepy—the pep pills have taken care of that.

We sit on the bed drinking and listening to the radio. God, I feel awful and I want to be alone, but she's here and I suppose I have to sleep with her—oh damn.

Denise goes on gazing into space; she hasn't spoken a word since we came in. The bottle falls to the floor and she leans back against the wall. Her breasts jut under her jumper and desire floods into me. I want her and hate her for making me want her. I pull off her clothes and take her violently, like it was rape. Hate her. Hate her. Love her. It is finished. I fling away from her and she lies like a discarded doll. There's no more wine blast it! When I get drunk I usually end up with a chick, but why should this girl mean something to me? I want to be unmoved by everything—like a god.

Her hair is spread out on the pillow, soft as silk in my hands. Her breasts slope softly to dark nipples. I kiss her and she curls up against me, murmuring softly, "Be gentle this time, lover."

She will never understand.

# seven

AWFUL morning. I curse the wine-sex hangover. Damn
Denise and everything that makes me weak and contemptible. I want to die but I guess I'm condemned
to drag along to the dreary end.

*Woke up this morning, blues all round my head.*
*Woke up this morning, blues all round my bed.*
*Got to my feet, head felt like lead. . . .*

I try to focus through squinting eyes. On the table
sits the radio. Denise, the careless slut, has forgotten
it . . . or maybe left it for me. She's nice that way.
My fingers fumble and turn on the knob. A bloody
cheerful voice tells me what toothpaste I should use.
I lie back and listen to the housewives' serial. The
same square cat chasing the same dumb moll through
two thousand episodes and hasn't made it yet. I turn
to another station and hear the time. Half the day
gone, but still the rest to get through. Yesterday the
coming out . . . the golden girl on the beach. I was
supposed to see her some time? This afternoon!

I make it to the bathroom, step under the shower

and foam myself with someone's perfumed soap. This process soothes the mind-body pain of awakening to the dull ache of my ordinary gloom mood.

I walk back naked to my room. My black clothes are lying on the floor—protection against the light. I fling them on, zip myself up, and go out into the street.

The glare of the summer day dazzles my jailbird eyes and the heat is too intense for my jail-soft body. Light and heat bounce from the melting tar under my shoes and I begin to cook in these tight-fitting clothes. I cross to the shady side and keep in close against the wall, drifting along hunched in my bodgie shuffle. I never move different to this except when the cops are on my tail.

I catch a bus to the University and try to look casual as I saunter into the grounds. I have passed it a few times but not for eighteen months, when I saw it briefly through the bars of the police van on my way to Fremantle jail. The building is O.K., I suppose—reflection pool and tower with a blue-faced clock. The girl said four o'clock and it is still only two. God, the hours go more slowly even than in jail.

I stroll through a covered archway and across a park-like area towards the playing fields. Despite the heat of the day a number of youths and girls are vigorously hitting or kicking different shaped balls around. I try to avert my eyes and slope away towards the river, but even here the sporting spirit asserts itself in the shape of rowers exuding the team spirit from every pore as they dip and strain in their

long boats. God, how it all brings me back to the
Swanview Boys' Home. . . .

Spanish style buildings, cream walled with orange
tiles and broad playing grounds sloping to the river's
edge. I see the skinny unattractive kid I was slouching
on the cricket field, mooning about, homesick for a
paddock patch in a country town, and the carefree
Noongar kids who had no team spirit, only a sort of
native loyalty.

No clouds in the sky, no shade on the cricket field,
but they must play this futile game in the beating
heat. It will build up the boys' physique and take the
edge off their energy for other more natural pursuits.

Bowler bowls, batter swipes, backstop catches,
fielders sweat. Hell, how I detest team games of any
sort and cricket in particular. Most of the other kids
seem to take it seriously and yell at me when I miss
a catch or fail to hit the ball when it's my turn to bat.
"Who cares who wins?" I once asked. "It's only a
game." They thought I must be kidding, so I shut up
after that and endured it alone.

Blessed relief when the siren blares, startling the
pigeons from the chapel roof. The brother gets up
from his seat in the shade of a tree, the boys pull the
wickets, collect the bats and balls, and run to the
locker room.

Four rows of lockers, each row a different colour
—red, blue, yellow and green—belonging to the different teams. Each boy has a locker of his own and is
supposed to "take a pride in it". Off with our clothes,
charge for the shower room with towels around

middles and wait in line. "Sir", bald-headed and stout in his flapping religious habit, supervises the floor show, manipulates the control valve and swipes alike the too slow and the too quick with well-used strap —his duty for God. "Hurry up there. Next. Back there and wash your face. Next. Next. . . ." Two minutes under the cold stream. Water off for the soap. On again to wash it off. A quick wipe over and out, dodging to escape the strap.

Blues, greens, reds and yellows keep up the team spirit in four lines outside the dining-room. A mark against one boy is a mark against the team and the team will take it out on him. No talking. No fidgeting. "Stop that whispering there. Blues first today. March."

Blues file in, greens, yellows and reds in a single line along the wall. Each boy grabs a plate off the pile in the servery and holds it up for the soup, goes to his place and stands for Grace.

"Bless us O Lord and these thy gifts. . . ."

"Sit!"

What was it we used to sing?

> Mummy, daddy, take me away
> From this awful place one day.
> No more eating stew like glue,
> No more eating bread like lead.

Tea over, washing up is a team job too, then study time. The boys sit under the bright lights, heads bent over their books. A black-robed brother prowls up and down the rows of desks, strap at the ready for the shirker and the cheat.

63

Eight o'clock, over to the chapel for prayers. Bed time. Long rows of beds in team dormitories.

At last all is quiet except for the breathing of the sleeping boys. I slide out of bed and pull on my clothes, tiptoe on bare feet to a balcony that leads to the dark stairway going down to the washroom door. Pressed against the wall, I sidle to the bottom of the stairs. No sound. I make my way round the dark wing to the moonlit quadrangle. Must take a chance now and hope to reach the locker room building on the other side without being seen.

I scuttle across the quadrangle into the shadow of a pillar on the far side and pause for breath. So far so good. If I get caught it'll be six of the best on the behind for sure. Christ, I just remembered. Sometimes they lock the locker room door. Gee, hope I can get in.

A hasty fumbling and the door swings open. Inside all is shadowy, but there are tall windows and a sharp pattern of moonlight splashes on to the floor. Anything could be hiding in the pitch black around the lockers. It is a hot night but my teeth begin to chatter and my legs go shaky and shivery.

Perhaps I should go back. Nobody will have missed me yet. No. Got to get out of this place. Got to get out of it. I'm in for the strap tomorrow anyway when Dickie sees my sums. Got to nick off now. Out of this "yes, sir" "no, sir" dump with its team games and sickening vegetables and stew and bullying brothers.

The old boss is the worst of the lot. His strap doesn't hurt as much as Dickie's, but he's a stupid old goat. The kids reckon a mouse once ran up his trouser leg and fell down dead. Always yacking about how he's doing the best for us and how ungrateful we are and noticing if you don't go to Communion and then questioning us about our sins. Can't take it any more.

I get my jumper and sandals from my locker, put on the jumper, hold the sandals, find my way to another locker and pull out an ex-army water bottle. I'm set. Something cracks behind me. Terrified, I crouch and then squeeze into a locker, pulling the door shut. No one. A board contracting, I suppose. Out!

The paddock is moonlit and as bare as the quadrangle, but I am lucky so far. No one watches me— except the imagined one. I scamper from shadow to shadow, worm under the gate, leap up and race along the road.

I reach the shelter of some pine-trees, sit down, put on my sandals, then up and on again. I climb the low stone wall that marks the boundary of the school land and plod along the exposed road with only my shadow for company. I am too tired to run. The night breeze blows softly through the pines and I am filled with a dreamtime loneliness, but I am excited too. Once I get to the main road I will know my way home like a cat.

A car hums in the distance, its headlights two round, swelling moons. I get off the road and crouch against the thick scrub. The hum becomes a roar, and the headlights blaze, tearing away the roadside shadows. With a shrill of brakes the car skids to a stop, doors fly open, and two black-robed figures leap out and grab.

"What's the meaning of this? Where do you think you're going? You cut that out now and get into the car."

I am pushed into the back seat and we zoom off . . . back to the beginning.

I don't care. Don't care. Don't care. They can do what they like with me now. At least I showed them, didn't I?

I am marched into the principal's office.

"So you were trying to abscond, my boy. A nice way of thanking us for all our trouble and care. The best is not good enough for you it seems. Do you mean to tell me you don't like it here?"

"I don't know, sir."

"If you were feeling unhappy why didn't you come to me and we could have had a little chat? You realize you have caused us a great deal of worry to-night."

"I don't care."

"So that's your attitude."

A hand jerks out and slaps my face.

"Why did you run away?"

No answer.

"You had the forethought to take your jumper, I see."

Old Dickie has shown up now.

"We'll soon warm you up, my boy, ha, ha. And what's this you've got here? A water bottle, eh? I suppose you brought a picnic lunch as well?"

"No, sir."

"What did you think you were going to eat?"

"I suppose some fruit from people's orchards, sir."

"Not only planning to run away, but planning to steal as well! Do you realize, my boy, that many a sorry life of crime has begun in this way?"

Old Dickie is getting carried away but the boss nods and glances at the door.

"Thank you, brother."

Dickie hitches up his habit and goes out. The boss opens a drawer and pulls out a strap.

"I hate to do this, my boy, but it is my duty to teach you right from wrong. I would be failing badly if I did not punish you for your behaviour tonight. Remember though that it will hurt me more than it will hurt you. Now bend over that chair."

I bite my lips to hold back the tears as six blows land on my undefended rump.

"You may go now. And remember to say your prayers."

In bed at last I bury my head in my pillow to stifle my sobs. A light is clicked on and I feel a brother standing over me. I lie rigid, pretending sleep, and the light clicks off.

Bastards! I'll never say another prayer as long as I live. I don't care. Don't care. . . .

Depressed by these memories I wander back to find the Espresso bar where I am supposed to meet the girl. Students pass to and fro, some alone and earnest with books under their arms, others in groups or pairs, laughing, discussing, chattering. I try to hear what they say:

67

"But surely Kafka was the greater misanthrope?"

Greater than who? And what is a misanthrope? I read a book by this writer in jail. It was queer but I could dig it in a way. I follow the group to the coffee shop and one of them holds open the door expecting me to come in. I shake my head and stand outside, the hair bristling on my body like a scared alley cat in a strange joint. I'll be out of my element in there. Way, way out of my depth. Better beat it before the girl turns up and it's too late to save my face.

I wonder why I have come. Curiosity perhaps, but then I am past being curious, because that is surely to hope that something might be different and I am past hope. Because I think they might be interesting? But then do I want or expect to be interested in anything? Perhaps to prove to the girl and to myself that I have guts, that I am really not afraid of anything. I have no hope and no ambition but I have trained myself to be self-sufficient, self-controlled, and I am in this way superior to the world of struggling, deluded fools of which all these people are a part.

"Come on, man," I urge myself. "Straighten up and walk in like a regular customer. Play it cool, not inferior to anyone."

I push open the swing door.

# eight

INSIDE, I stand acting the big shot phoney and take a long look around. Groups of people, mostly students I guess, sit at small tables. Some look the ordinary nondescript city types, but most of them are what I suppose they call bohemians, the girls in casual slacks and jumpers, some of the men with beards and dark-rimmed spectacles, almost all in corduroys and open shirts. Chinese looking lanterns drop from the ceiling like big white moons. Through the far door is a court-yard where there are more tables under bright beach umbrellas, but the shop itself is not very big or speci-ally grand.

One wall is papered with yellowed pages of old text books, the others hung with paintings like no-thing I've ever seen or felt, although a notice says it is an exhibition of recent Australian works. But then I suppose I'm not what they call Australian. I'm just an odd species of native fauna cross-bred with the migrant flotsam of a goldfield.

There is no juke-box here, only some sneaky classic-type music trickling from an unseen source. Foreign territory for me, though no one seems to notice it but myself. This is funny because most places I go, outside the gang hangouts, I usually create some sort of hostile or suspicious interest that inflates my ego. Maybe the girl only picked this place on purpose to belittle me somehow. Well, I can't let her get away with that. Who does she think she is? I'll find a table and sit like I'm used to it, drinking coffee and smoking until she comes. Or maybe best wait outside for a bit. The second time in is never so bad . . . like jail. Exit the big shot.

Still an hour to wait. I feel I need something to add to myself. I pluck up courage and ask a timid looking chap how far it is to the nearest pub. He tells me about ten minutes walk and points the way, so with a purpose in mind I stride it out.

I try not to act nervous as I wait at the bar. I guess my time in jail has matured me so that I might easily pass for twenty-one, but has it really toned down my skin colour as much as I think? If the barman takes me for a half-caste, he has a right to challenge me to produce my exemption ticket. As a quadroon I would be eligible for this, but in applying for it I would be found out for under-age drinking and they could put me in for that. Most native boys I know start their jail education by being put in on a drinking charge, but I bet half the Uni boys in here are under twenty-one. I don't see anyone challenging them, and if they did I can't see them being sent to jail. These two at the end of the bar have started up an argument about football scores and one of them seems properly hostile. He has a belligerent look in his popping blue eyes and his big punch-packing fists begin to clench. I thought it was only natives were supposed to get fighting drunk.

The barman comes my way at last and I order a beer. He serves me matter of fact. Good old prison— I've passed. I drink enough for courage and walk back. Still half an hour to go by the tower clock.

I notice there is a bookshop near the coffee place. A book would give me a front. Might even make me pass for a student. I go in and stand bewildered among the racks and tables piled with literature. What to choose? Nothing expensive. Maybe one of these highbrow looking paper-backs. I take one from the rack. *Crime and Punishment.* Funny, I read that in jail. Good yarn. *War and Peace. Anna Karenina.* Hell! Fancy finding them here too.

I pass on to a section marked Psychology and dig about like a dog unearthing juicy bones. My cup of tea, but too expensive. Time is moving on. Drama. *Waiting for Godot.* I open it at random.

"We wait. We are bored. No, don't protest, we are bored to death, there's no denying it. Good. A diversion comes along and what do we do? We let it go to waste. Come let's get to work! In an instant all will vanish and we'll be alone again, in the midst of nothingness."

This looks all right.

I make my purchase and walk back to the coffee shop. With drink and book for armour I enter with more confidence, order a coffee at the counter and take it to a corner table. Easy, wasn't it? No one takes any notice of me at all. I sip with an eye on the door and minutes drip by. Sip, minute, sip. Pull out a cigarette. Puff, minute, puff. No girl yet, but don't panic. Go on playing it cool. Don't like this music much. These little bitty tunes make you phoney calm. Rock, straightforward blast and blare gets you raw and jagged. Like crazy, like life.

Myself mocks myself. Read your book, man. That's the way.

"Let's go."
"We can't."
"Why not?"
"We're waiting for Godot."

The door swings and she is here at last—the girl from the lazy afternoon. She is wearing a pair of skin-tight black slacks that crease at the knees as she walks and the sloppy sweater reaching past her hips makes her seem fragile and small. I feel a sudden emptiness. The urge to see her has been satisfied and I want to go.

I sit blank-faced waiting for her to notice me. Out of an eye corner I see her turn a complete circle. She knows everyone it seems, and calls "Hullo" as she goes by. How different from me: I couldn't ever call out to anyone or move sort of easy like that.

The Hullo jive is finally over and she comes to my corner with four boy friends in tow. She's friendly casual like before.

"Hullo. I hoped you'd turn up."

"I thought I might as well."

She turns to the others. "This is the boy I told you about. The one I met on the beach."

I take a deep drag on my cigarette. Nerves, but I

eye them straight. Some of them look like queers, but I could be wrong. Maybe that's just the look they get round here. Anyway they are a new sort to me. I make a motion of accepting them, but I am on my guard. They sit at my table and I hear them call the girl June. They order coffee and she talks to me. Trying to make me feel at ease, I guess, but I am tongue-tied and miserable as hell. What did she tell them about me? That I am coloured and an ex-con? Does that make me interesting? A sort of curiosity?

"Frank and Bill are doing Social Anthropology," June says, like reading my mind. "I thought you might be able to give them some fresh slants."

"Why?" I ask.

"Oh, because you seem to have ideas and you're not afraid to express yourself."

Frank is a thin, intense looking chap with a neat dark beard. Bill has a round smooth face with a stuck on smile. They look at me and I look back at them.

"So what?" I say. "What do you want to know?"

"We wondered for instance, whether you might have any personal views on this Austral Grove experiment? I mean, do you consider it a good idea—a sort of stepping-stone from camp life into the general community?"

I listen to their bull-dust questions and I hear myself make the sort of answers they expect. . . . Yes, I have been to the Grove a few times. It might work out. Some of them are really trying to make the grade. Drink a problem of course. . . .

The other part of my mind mocks the phoney words. . . .

73

A problem all right. Getting onto the stuff to start with. Can't trust just anyone. Might be a police pimp laying a trap. Got to know a good sympathetic white to buy the grog and sell it back to you for double the price. If you can't find him, wood alcohol, metho and so forth will do. Doesn't taste so good, but gets you drunk quicker and costs less.

I remember the last time I was there. Found an empty hut with broken window-panes and settled down with a bottle of cheap sweet wine. Some of the men came in with a few more bottles and the women gathered round like flies. A big full-blood gin cottoned onto me.

"Give us a drink, yeller feller. Just a little one and I'll be nice to you. . . . Come on. . . . Jesus, that was good. Just one more. Come on. . . ."

Shrieks of laughter, sound of breaking bottles, angry argument and drunken couplings. . . . Warm brown breasts and heavy nipples rising and falling in drunken sleep. . . . I staggered out, vomited and stumbled to a tap. . . .

This Bill is still talking with his all's-right-with-the-world smile. "It is obvious of course," he says, "that given ordinary decent conditions they would behave like ordinary decent citizens."

"I know," I agree, as though it is as simple as that. I don't even know how his "ordinary decent citizens" behave or whether they exist at all.

A thin blue-stocking kind of girl with big specs and straight short hair pulls up her chair and listens earnestly.

"What I always think," she comes in, "it's not the

74

natives need educating so much. It's the whites."

I guess from the way she looks at me that this is the closest she ever got to an Aboriginal. She offers me this chewed old bit of white corn as though expecting me to seize on it with pleased surprise. How broad-minded, how perceptive to express a big, brave thought like that! I try to think of something wither-ing, but all I can come up with is: "You're kidding!"

She doesn't take it for sarcasm. In fact it stimulates her no end.

"Indeed, I'm not," she says. "I feel very strongly on this point. I think it's quite arrogant and stupid of us to want to drag the Aborigines into our so called 'civilized' society. Why can't we leave them alone? They have such wonderful beliefs and customs of their own. It's not as if we had anything better to offer them. Don't you agree?"

"Sure," I say and she fixes me with a fascinated stare. Maybe she thinks if she keeps it up long enough I will leap out and do a corroboree in the middle of the floor.

The others seem to realize that the polite possibili-ties of this subject are about exhausted and the con-versation veers from me. I half listen as they rave on about last term's lectures, musical recitals I have never heard, plays I have never seen, books I have never read. I sit back mute and hide my feelings behind a cynical smile.

They've got onto art now, comparing, praising, de-fending, condemning this artist and that.

"I see you're looking at Dorian's masterpiece," June

says suddenly, nodding towards a picture on the near wall. "What do you make of it?"

I hadn't registered to it before, except to note that it was called for some reason "Man in Revolt of Exile". I can't see any man, only a revolting mess of hectic semi-circles and triangles, but I have been listening enough now to get a line on this art jazz.

"It seems to hit something in me," I say. "There's a certain mood of—well, melancholy, going off into utter, black despair."

They all stop talking and give me the floor.

"I'd say it was a sort of battle between light and dark. The dark nearly wins, but the fight goes on. Towards the centre there is this glow of hope, but very faint of course. Here and there it flares up into a rage, but that gets submerged in these sort of frustrated angles. I'd say the whole thing has a kind of jagged rhythm." The artist chap called Dorian sits listening intently.

"Or am I being too psychological?" I ask.

"No, no, not at all," Dorian says eagerly. "The whole thing's intensely psychological. Rage, anger, despair, frustration—they're all in it as you say. I was in a funny mood when I painted it and you've interpreted it very well. Do you paint too by any chance?"

"No," I say. "I hardly do anything except sit and think."

Dorian seems pretty much my way now. He points out another picture that he says he painted in protest against interference with the natural bush in King's Park. This art jargon is a pushover once you have the key to the artist's mind, so I do pretty well with this one too.

This leads to a heated discussion about whether some of the Park should be converted into sports grounds.

"What do you think about it?" June asks me.

I have no interest in the subject and no views on it at all, but I suppose I have to say something.

"Sport is a bore and the bush is a bore too, but at least nature is a natural bore so why not leave it alone?"

They all laugh at this though I had not intended it to be funny. I was just answering as truthfully as I could. Anyway, I seem to have been a success with this mob. They ask me a few friendly-curious questions about myself, where I come from, how long I have been in Perth, and what my main interests are. I can see June has not let on about the jail part for some reason and I am about to tell them myself. I mean, why not? It is enough of a drag to have been in jail without having to pretend I haven't. But June cuts in quick.

"He only got here yesterday," she says; "doesn't know many people yet, but his hobby is jazz. I mean—" she turns to me—"you've made a special study of it, haven't you?"

They ask me about it and I talk back some of the book stuff I have read. Jazz, the negro art, evolved in the plantations, in slavery and exile and misery. Triumph of the human spirit. The only valid new art to arise in this century. The only worth while thing to come out of America. They ask me about the

Australian Aborigines, whether they could ever produce an art to rival jazz. I don't know much about
the Aborigines or how they feel, but I have a shot at
answering. "For one thing," I say, "they wouldn't
have a chance against the imported stuff. It's big
business now and anything home grown would be
kept off the market. But, anyway, the Aborigines
wouldn't be interested. If there's money to be made
from their music the whites will use and debase it to
suit their ends, until there's nothing left in it of the
black man's soul."

Dorian says he thinks jazz is fascinating too and
asks me to a party in his loft tonight. The others all
seem to be going, so I say O.K. I don't know why,
because I don't really want to go. Or maybe I do.
They're not my crowd, but I suppose they're trying
to make me feel at home and they're interesting in a
way.

It's time to leave now and I follow them out. June
puts a hand on my arm.

"I've got to go now," she says, "but I'll see you
tonight."

She tells me how to get to the loft and hopes I enjoyed the afternoon. I tell her it was quite an experience to meet some real, big intellectuals.

"You can hold your own with them pretty well,
can't you?" she says. I think she means it in a friendly
way and I smile down at her to save answering. Then
I watch her move away across the lawn, calling out
to a friend with that easy belonging voice of hers.

# nine

IT's early evening time and my stomach's empty except for the coffee and the grog. I make for a Greek café back in town. It is stinking hot inside and the greasy three-course meal is no better or worse than I expect. I gulp it down without enjoyment and without disgust.

My hunger sated, I buy a paper to read the time away till eight o'clock. I turn automatically to the police court news. One acquaintance has been arrested for breaking and entering, two others for attempted rape, and the police have promised an all-out drive to put down the bodgie element. I turn the pages until only the table top remains to be read, its blotches and stains a sickening story of many horrible meals.

I wonder whether I still consider myself a member of this bodgie element. I don't want to belong to them any more. They are a pack of morons. Clueless, mindless idiots. What about this other mob? No good pretending I could ever belong with them, even if I imagined life would be any better if I did. Maybe they are really as bored in their way as I am in mine and I amused them for a moment or two being like different. That chap Dorian was a fool really. It didn't occur to him I wasn't talking about his bloody awful picture, only about myself. Even that whisper of hope I talked about was me. If I let up a minute on my mental discipline it creeps in again suggesting there might be something in life besides absurdity—even a hint of meaning. I have to shut it out because it is a liar. It is the most dangerous illusion of all. Except maybe love!

Another hour to this damn party. Will I go or not, and if not, where? Back to the milk-bar gang? Pay good cash to see the glorious fakery of blown-up life from the United States of Utopia? Not on your life! I could go to the public library perhaps and pinch a book to take back to my dingy little room. I remember the book in my pocket. Not bad, the bits I read of it. Not about anything much except a sort of senseless onward dying. Like life.

I take it out and dip into it again.

"No, no. We could start all over again perhaps."
"That should be easy."
"It's the start that's difficult."
"You can start from anything."
"Yes, but you have to decide."
"True. . . ."

Hell, don't say there's a sermon wrapped up in this somewhere! Maybe not. . . .

"That's the idea, let's ask each other questions."
"What do you mean, at least there's that?"
"That much less misery."
"True."

"Well? If we gave thanks for our mercies?"
"What is terrible is to have thought."
"But did that ever happen to us?"
"Where are all these corpses from?"
"These skeletons."
"Tell me that."
"True. . . ."

Good stuff this. Not even pretending to make sense but making it. Eyes read on and mind looks through some backroom window at a miserable boy on a sagging bed stacked with shabby paper-backs. Chair, wardrobe, rickety table, suitcase spilling out unwashed clothes, empty tins in dusty corners, empty bowl on a mass of half burned papers in a blackened fireplace, glossy black cockroach scuttling over a pink nude in an open magazine, dust particles floating like tiny worlds in a beam of sunlight from a window, lean cat silhouetted for a moment against the light. Three hungry days. No coin and tomorrow the rent. . . .

Brrrh . . . brrrh . . . alarm noises shatter his sleep. He slaps at the clock and yawns, his mind slowly absorbing the fact that it is time for action.

Cold hands tidy dishevelled clothes, pull on muddy boots and long black duffle coat, pocket a screw-driver and a cosh.

His feet move reluctantly down the dark passage-way and out the front door. He's got to go through with it now. Got to get coin and some new threads. Nothing to worry about. Cased the joint yesterday. Should be a pushover.

Raining and the night is moonless, starless, bleak.

The best kind of night for a bust. Drops fall on his face, the trees sough and rock in a reeling jive. A lull and the trees seem to wait. Next number starts with a frantic rush and the dance goes on, moan of wind sax, drumming of striking teeming rain, flapping and twisting of wild demon shapes.

The youth moves quietly, hood pulled up over his head, raindrops on eyelashes turning the street lights into rainbow shining gems. Running water splashes over his boot tops, soaks his socks and clamps his jeans damply to long native shanks.

Swell night, real dark and everything fresh like new from the rain. Real beautiful in a way, all aheave with the storm. Real crazy-mad night for a night cat, too numb to feel the cold. He feels belonging in this dark, not like in the day, outcast and naked. Nigger-nigger-go-away-day.

Avenue ends at the shopping centre and not a soul about. Faint light through a plate glass window. He peers inside, making out counter and stacked shelves. Grouse night. Everything's grouse, except how the hell to reach the back of this place.

He remembers a narrow alley and makes around to it, keeping close to the darker side. Loitering with intent! Hands feel out a six foot corrugated iron gate and clutch the top. Edge hurts but is too blunt to cut. One foot on block and padlock. He heaves up and straddles. Gate creaks. He drops, sinks into soft mud and crouches, listening with panting breath. Nothing but the rain and the wind. Desert boots ruined, but otherwise everything going fine. Hard for him to make out the selected shop from this side. He peers through a small window towards a faint light—no one there. Store-room stacked with cardboard cartons, faintly lit through panelled glass door of the front shop.

He feels round the small window and finds that the putty is rotting and flaking off. If the pane was out he might be able to reach the half-turned key in the back door. Screw-driver swipes off putty and jerks out tacks. He slips the jemmy edge under the pane and eases the glass until it is almost free. Good. Just one last little jab. Crash! Shatter of glass on metal. Hell! He freezes and crouches with nerves strung tight. Faint sound on sensitive ear-drums. Someone turning in bed. Probably some lousy Jew who counts his money every night!

Hand reaches through the window, fumbles towards the key and pulls it out. Hard to turn. Ah! That's got it. He slips through and shuts the door, pauses inside, dripping water from drenched clothes, face hot and feet icy cold. He peers about, mind and body alert. Door into the shop unlocked. Enters warily, remembering the odd night cop.

He finds the cash drawer on the counter and forces the cheap lock. Stuffs notes and silver into deep pockets and darts swiftly to collect sharp clothes. Finds an empty carton and shoves them inside.

Grouse! Fifty quid at least and all these new threads. Rent taken care of and money over for sharp shoes. Swingiest cat in town!

Off now before the luck runs out. Locks the back door and leaves the key in for kicks. Everything swell. No rain now to wet the loot. Damn! He's lost the bloody cosh! Hopes it's dropped in the mud so they won't find fingerprints. Cops haven't got his prints yet anyway, so should be safe enough. The night is a friend to the night cat. Nobody sees. . . .

The Town Hall clock strikes eight. Party is on in the loft! I go on reading.

"Let's pass on now to something else, do you mind?"
"I was just going to suggest it."
"But to what?"
"Ah!"
"Suppose we got up to begin with."
"No harm in trying."
"Child's play."
"Simple question of will-power."
"And now?"
"Help!"
"Let's go."
"We can't."
"Why not?"
"We're waiting for Godot."

To go or not to go? Read on.

"All the dead voices."
"They make a noise like wings."
"Like leaves."
"Like sand."
"Like leaves."

Might find a clue in this crazy stuff.

"Leaves?"
"In a single night."
"It must be spring."
"But in a single night!"
"I tell you we weren't here yesterday. Another of your nightmares."

"And where were we yesterday evening according to you?"

"How do I know? In another compartment. There's no lack of void."

"Good. We weren't here yesterday evening. Now what did we do yesterday evening?"

"Do?"

"Try and remember."

Denise. Dark hair on the pillow. Soft like silk. Waiting in the milk-bar now I guess. Keep out of that old trap, man, just for tonight. She likes you and she makes you soft. And what about that June doll? What about her? Don't know. Don't care, but might as well find out—for kicks.

# ten

A DINGY lane leads to the party place. Muffled jazz beats the air that has swapped today's heat for the different animal heat of night. A sea breeze cools me a little as I stand wondering how to get in . . . night-time, play-time, cool-time is wonderful.

A few others drift along and I go in with them. The music wails louder as we climb the stairs and are drawn into a room pulsating with rhythm and life. It's like a bodgie party in a way, but not really like. This mob is different, forcing the mood, too much high-brow talk, not drifting easily with the jazz current like the milk-bar gang. I feel like out of place, an outsider looking in, no part of this set-up. But now I'm here I guess I'll have to act out the night.

It's a broad low loft, the walls plastered over with unframed daubs, mostly in the same style as Dorian's psychological masterpiece in the Uni coffee shop. I turn my back on the room and fake the big-shot art critic, thinking culture thoughts. Dorian spots me and comes skidding across the room. He slaps me on the shoulder and calls me "mate".

"Come over and have a grog," he says. "There's beer and wine. Take your pick. I'm doing a fantastic picture I'd like to discuss with you, but got to get this party kicking on first."

We down a beer together and the atmosphere of the place starts to grow on me. I begin to dig it in a way.

"Good boy! You came."

I look round and June is there. She has on the same rig as the afternoon and I am glad. It would be awful if she was togged up flash. She sees me looking at her clothes.

"No time to go home and change," she says. "I lead a dog's life."

"Yeah?"

"First party I've been to in months."

"Why?"

"One does have to work sometimes to pass exams, you know."

"I wouldn't know."

"It's a pity. You'd make a good student."

"You're kidding."

"No really. You've got the brains. You did Junior by correspondence, didn't you?"

"Yeah, in jail. How did you know?"

"Someone in the Department checked for me. He said you did a pretty brilliant pass."

"So what? It killed the time."

"Ever feel like going on with it?"

"What's the use?"

"There are such things as scholarships."

Sure I've got brains and sure there are scholarships. I could blind this mob with science. Why not? Because it's too late. Too late from the day I was born I guess.

"You've mugged up all this psychology," I say. "Why can't you understand?"

"Understand what?" she asks.

"What makes people tick who don't think your way."

"That's what psychology tries to teach us," she says.

"Schizophrenia, dypsomania, nymphomania, hydrophobia, paranoia. . . ."

She laughs easily. "All those things you suffer from? Like reading a medical book and finding you have symptoms of everything. You've had a lot of bad breaks and you've built up your own sort of defence against life. Otherwise you're as normal as they come."

I search for words to explain the unexplainable.

"Wanting to win games and races, get top in exams, the competitive spirit, getting up and on—you'd say that was normal, I guess?"

"It's human nature," she says.

"What do you call it if you just don't dig this success jazz? Or maybe dig it in a way, but not really inside you? That human nature?"

"Of a kind, yes."

"Of another kind, see? My kind."

She's a nice doll this one. I even think she believes there's not all that difference between her sort and mine.

"Anyway, who cares?" I down another beer. "Let's dance before I feel sober."

We move into the centre and are swept away with the old life force pulsing from a black man's horn, weeping, wailing, laughing, loving. Mind blank to everything but rhythm and sound. Rhythm and girl. Getting to like this doll. Might even like her a lot. Mind and body heat with desire. Phoney emotion. Phoney crowd. Rich daddies and faking life. Got no place here. Don't want to stay.

". . . jazz as an art form," Dorian says to his partner as we pass.

I think he's telling someone the bull I put over in the coffee shop. Phoney stuff but this mob will swallow anything. The black man's jazz has got them like it's got me, but give it a name and they can fake they've put it in its place, put it back where it belongs. The master race, and all that crap. Got to show this girl they can't put it over me. Walk out on her when I like. Snap the fingers, just like that.

Music stops and she throws back her head.

"I'll say you can dance," she says.

Damn her. Not the colour so much . . . the way I move . . . more supple than a white boy. . . .

"You'll be all right now, won't you? You know most of the crowd."

"They're a phoney mob," I say. "The bodgies are better any day."

I want her to mind but she laughs and pats my arm. The music starts up again and another bloke swings away with her.

I get a drink and stand about listening to the talk.

89

Phrases blur in my mind, twist and weave patterns of no account. Word associations rise like bubbles, break and dissolve in air. I flop on the floor with a glass of wine and smoke the long white sadness of a cigarette.

A girl sits down beside me. I don't look at her. Don't say anything. She can come crawling and I will reject her. Cool, like a god.

"You're with this jazz, aren't you? It means a lot to you."

I thought it was June, but it's some other broad.

"Nothing means anything to me. I dig it, that's all."

"It must mean something to you then."

She is a fool.

"Meaning is an illusion," I say.

"Don't you believe in anything—nothing at all?" She is drunk and leans against me with half-closed eyes.

"What is belief?" I ask.

"Got to believe in something," she says.

"Like God and all that supernatural jazz?"

She wrinkles up her face. "Not God. Things like freedom, equality, rights of the common man."

I grind out the butt of my cigarette. "They are the absurdest illusions of all—except love."

"Don't you believe in love?"

"Love is lust."

"Then you must believe in lust."

"Don't believe in anything, only jazz. Jazz is love and love is lust and lust is nothing. So nothing is anything."

Oh hell! Who cares about love and lust and jazz?

I lapse into silence and look at her through the smoke of another cigarette.

A man drifts into my vision, smoke clears and I see that it is Dorian.

"What about that picture?" he says. "I'd like to know what you think of it."

I look vaguely around the walls.

"Which one?"

"It's downstairs as a matter of fact."

The girl hooks her arm through mine. "Go away," she says. "He's my baby."

He ignores her. "I'd like your advice on a title actually. We could discuss it after the others go." He looks at me intently under drooping lids. "I want to get something cosmic into it."

Suddenly my senses clear. My moment of clarity in drink has come. Everything stands out stark and separate.

"Call it *A Queer World*," I say. "That ought to fit all right."

The girl giggles. Dorian gives me a long strange look and drifts off to another group.

"You don't approve of poor Dorian," the girl says. "Right, darling?"

"Wrong," I say. "To disapprove of something means that I must approve of something else. It means that I must believe in right and wrong, but I don't. Both are illusions."

"Your philosophy fascinates me," she says. "Tell me more."

I seem to be thinking clear thoughts and search for clear words.

"Nothing is right; nothing is wrong. Everything exists in itself and by itself. All things are separate and alien from each other."

She snuggles closer.

"I don't feel alien from you right now."

"All things are alien from me. I am rejected and I stand utterly alone. Nothing is mine or belongs to me and I belong nowhere in this world or the next."

"Then you believe in a next world?"

"I believe in nothing and nobody. There is no refuge or comfort anywhere for me."

We lapse into silence and I listen to the fragments of conversation floating to and fro against the rhythm of the canned jazz.

" 'They make a noise like wings,' " I murmur sadly. " 'A noise like feathers, like leaves, like ashes, like sand.' "

"Are you a poet?" she asks.

"That was a quotation," I tell her.

"What does it mean?"

"Nothing and everything," I say. "Like ashes, like love, like sand, like life."

"Poor lonely darling," she says and begins to cry.

"You're drunk," I say.

"Beautiful boy, we are both so beautifully drunk and this little girlie wants to go outside."

She gets up, staggering. I take her arm and we stumble out together. She knows where the place is and then she says: "Don't let's go back. Come in here and talk a bit."

She pushes open a door and I feel for a switch. "Don't need any light," she says.

I understand her now. She pulls me down with her onto a bed and sighs as her arms twist round my neck. My body is as warm as hers but my mind is detached and cold. This time I don't feel anything like hate or love. Only feel sick. I throw off her stranglehold and fling myself out the door.

A trumpet blares a cynical laughing tune as I run out into the lane. The buildings sway inwards on either side. The ground writhes under my feet. I look up and the sky is blurred with reeling stars. Nothing stable and true in all the universe. The footpath rises and sends me sprawling on hands and knees. I get up and struggle on. . . . Like ashes, like sand, like life . . . no refuge anywhere.

# III
# RETURN

# eleven

STOP running. What's the hurry? No place to go anyway. Just walk on. Not to somewhere, to anywhere.

The lights of the milk-bar draw me across the road.
In the doorway, I hesitate. At the end of one dark
journey, why start on another?

Two short steps into this place and where will they
end? Who will I meet in there and where will the
meeting lead? . . . "Boys, boys learn to avoid the
occasions of sin. Keep away from bad company as
you would keep out of an all-consuming fire."

While mind draws back, body takes the fatal step.

No sign of Denise or anyone else I know much. I
sit at a table by myself and watch the make-believe-
they-are-alive kids moving like zombies to the juke-
box will.

I look around the familiar whitewashed walls as
though for the first time—names scribbled in chalk
or lipstick, lovers' names encircled by diseased hearts.
Over there a red wine stain like a misshapen cross, red
drops streaming from the arms. Blurred vision of

agony. Bitter taste of defeat, the vinegar of futility.

This bloody place, the occasion of discovery. This table, the one where the youth that was me sat that afternoon on his seventeenth birthday, sucking up coke, relaxed, not expecting anything. . . .

"Hi, man, where'd you get those sharp new shoes?"

"Father Christmas put them in my stocking."

The door opens and a man comes in. He stands thick-set, hard eyes taking in the room, moving from table to table, face to face. The attendant puts down his paper, talk drops to a murmur and the juke-box stops dead.

The youth sucks and slouches, playing it cool. He glances out the door. Rain splashing in the street, swirling down the gutters, bouncing off a big black car beside the kerb. . . . The cop could be after any-one in here. It wouldn't be him, he hasn't skited to a soul about the bust. Nothing else they could have on him—unless they found the cosh.

He gets to his feet, like bored, fumbles for a coin and drifts over to the music box. Rainbow lights flash as he touches the switch. He scans the song list casu-ally. . . . That stolen stuff in his room, nice and ready for them to find. Good job he's spent most of the money.

A heavy hand falls on his shoulder and he swings round. The big man turns the collar of his coat and flashes a badge.

"I'm a police officer. Come along with me, please."

The youth shrugs violently, but the clasp is firm.

"How about one last little number like, before we go?"

"Come on. Get moving. I haven't got all day."

He answers with a what-the-hell gesture to the crowd, and goes out, joined hand to shoulder with the cop.

The rain has ceased but a few big drops hit hard and cold as they cross the footpath to the waiting car. The detective pushes in after him in the front seat and the driver cop starts up. The rain pours down again in an angry burst. Windscreen wipers swish-swish, click-click, clearing two watery arcs through which the road curves like a black monster rearing out of the sea. Swish-swish, clicketty-click, juke-box baby seventeen.

The theme clicks over in his head through the long days before the trial. He sits at last waiting his turn on a bench against a passage wall, fat policeman at the exit, barred window at the other end.

Juke-box baby seventeen, graduated and got that twist. Seventeen, seventeen. Juke-box baby seventeen.

Real grouse birthday this. First time he's had a party. Crazy celebration. Big thrill. Going to get what he deserves—a real big present at last. . . . Payment for the cosh they found in the lane, the things in his room, the knife under his pillow. . . . Gone, man, real gone. . . . And may they rot in hell!

Seventeen, seventeen, graduated and stood his trial. Real big kicks at seventeen. . . .

"Right, boy. Your turn."

Gee, that fat old square Robinson's turned up again.

Thought he'd be content with the statement, but no, here he is in court. Dear old guardian angel probation officer. What a trouble the youth's been to him since he chucked that nice job, and started flitting from hostel to rented room, from rented room to rented room.

"Now listen to me," he says. "Don't get smart with the magistrate. No lip, understand? No talking unless you're spoken to. Remember to answer his questions politely with a 'Sir' and you should be all right. I'll be behind you all the time."

They go in and the cop plonks himself down inside the door. The defendant sits at a table beside old Robinson, long-haired youth and pudgy man. . . . The youth wishes they'd let him sit alone so he could be the centre of attention. Like Marlon Brando, real tough bodgie mumbling out the side of his mouth.

The special Juvenile Magistrate trots in, trying to stride importantly. No good. He hasn't the height to command respect. The court rises, the youth rises and towers over the lot of them. The magistrate moves to the bench and sits on a stool that is raised by two fat legal tomes. He sits. The court sits.

Impressive silence broken by a snigger. Jehovah glares. Guardian angel's wing digs defendant in the ribs. Business begins.

The cop who arrested him takes the oath. Exhibits —cosh, knife, stolen clothes—to be examined later by the Magistrate. Detective sits. Guardian angel is summoned and flaps to his feet.

"Your Honour, the Child Welfare Department has had trouble with the defendant ever since he left

Swanview, where he was sent at the age of nine, after being charged and found guilty of breaking and entering. There he received a fair education and the annual reports showed him to be not unintelligent. You have the Department's report on this matter, sir. At the beginning of last year, he was released and placed under my guidance. The Department found him a good position in a reputable firm and accommodation in a boys' hostel. Unfortunately, even with these advantages, he failed to make good. He moved from the hostel and left his job without my knowledge. I lost contact with him until I was notified by the police that he had been picked up on a car stealing charge. He was committed to the juvenile section of the jail for a term of six months. After his release, I again found him a job and respectable lodgings, but he again eluded me. I understand that then he went to live in a Native Settlement where he consorted with some of the most undesirable elements. He is of part aboriginal descent and this appears to have made him acceptable there. After some weeks, he left the camp and rented a room in the city, but he did not reform or try to find a job. Instead, he frequented a milk-bar, which is known to the police as a breeding place of crime. I have stated that he is intelligent and could quite easily find work if he wanted to, but he spurns all efforts to help him and I honestly believe him to be one of the most difficult types to deal with. Sir, may I hand you the statement which he dictated to me at the Receiving Home?"

He passes up two typewritten sheets of paper. The Magistrate adjusts his glasses and puts on an expres-

sion of deep concentration. Traffic noises filter into
the room. A cop shuffles his heavy feet. Coughs echo
intermittently. Asthmatic breathings wheeze about.

The Magistrate relaxes his brow and looks up. "Will
the defendant take the stand, please."

There is no stand. It means he must stand out in
front.

"You say in your statement that you do not believe
in God?"

"Yeah."

A nudge from the probation officer.

"Yes, sir."

"So you do not want to be sworn in on the Bible?"

"No, I don't."

"Will you give your word of honour then, to speak
the truth?"

"How can I?"

A nudge from Mr Robinson.

"Yes, sir."

"That's better. Why did you commit the crime?"

The youth clutches wildly at a thread of hope.
"Couldn't get a job and had no money. I needed the
dough for food and rent."

"Did you try to find work?"

"No."

"And why did you steal the clothes?"

"All mine were shabby and out of date so I couldn't
mix with the mob. You know they look down on you
if you don't look sharp."

"I hope you will answer this question correctly
now. Do you feel any guilt for what you have done?"

"No. I was starving and my rent was due. That

square had what I wanted and more than I did. Those people lived in luxury."

"What does the word 'square' mean?"

"Oh, ordinary people, them that like work and that."

"You mean decent people, I presume." He consults the file again. "Your probation officer and the detective both state that you had in your room a large collection of lurid paper-backs—crime stories and so forth. Do you like reading this type of literature?"

"Before, I used to think they were terrif. But now they bore me. I don't read anything now."

"You frequent a certain milk-bar, I understand."

"Only place I could go after the camp, sir. It was tough there, always drinking and fighting. But at the milk-bar I could listen to the juke-box and talk."

"I understand that a certain class of youth known as 'bodgies' gather there. Do you call yourself a bodgie?"

I try to find an answer to that one.

"Do you?"

"No . . . sir."

"What do you call yourself?"

"A progressive dresser, I guess, sir."

"Oh, is there a difference?"

"I think so, sir. I mean. . . ."

"Perhaps the difference is that a bodgie carries a bike chain and a so-called progressive dresser carries a knife and cosh."

The Magistrate looks pointedly at the exhibits. It's a joke, and hollow laughter echoes through the court.

"You may step down now. The Court will be in

recess for ten minutes. Mr Robinson, will you come into my chambers, please."

Seventeen, seventeen, graduated and got that twist. Juke-box king ain't no square. Seventeen and second trial. . . .

The Magistrate returns.

"I have discussed the case with the defendant's probation officer and can see no mitigating circumstances. So far as I can make out there are no other matters to be taken into consideration and I feel it my duty to commit this youth to a further term of imprisonment. I sincerely hope it will be a lesson to him and to others."

He turns his pale blank face to the defendant. "I sentence you to eighteen months imprisonment with hard labour. While in the place of detention you will be given a psychological examination and treated if necessary."

Shrug it off, man. Big present. Eighteen lovely months, all found and plenty of good company. Old school mates complete with old school ties. . . . "Boys, boys, avoid the occasion of sin. Above all bad company!" Eighteen lovely, lousy months . . . all lost. May the dirty bastards burn in hell.

The defendant looks up as they take him outside. Racing clouds pile up over the last small patch of sky. He goes to the lavatory and vomits. His guardian angel offers him a cigarette. . . .

Someone claps me on the back.

"Hi, man!"

"Hi, man!" I parrot back. "How're you going?"

"Still out, anyway," he says.

I turn and see that it is Jeff, my prison-redeemed friend.

"Hi, man," I say again. "How's that swell big doll of yours?"

"She won't have a bar of me," he says. "She wants big money now."

"Yeah," I say. "Yeah. They get that way."

"But I want her like hell," he says.

"So what? You've got nothing coming to you. Nothing to confess."

He looks away. "I want her like hell."

"Yeah. Like leaves. Like spring."

"Eh, man?"

"Like hell. Like fire. Like life."

"Hey! You all right?"

"Yeah. Yeah, sure. You want this big doll. She wants big money. You ain't got her. You ain't got big money. So what?"

He sits down beside me, takes a rum bottle from his hip pocket and divides the remains of the grog into two cups.

"I don't know what to do, man," he says. "All the things we argued about in jail, God or no God. Christ-God, or phoney, or plain duped. Remember?"

"Yeah." I take a swig of the rum and look at the wine stain on the wall. "So what?"

"You've got more brains than me," he says. "More than anyone I get a chance of talking to. If you were dinkum—if you still reckon it's just a yarn they put over us so they can keep on top. . . ."

I look at him. That's what he wants me to tell him

because he wants this big doll and he wants to get hold of the money to pay for her.

I toss off the last of the rum and get up from the chair.

"You work that out for yourself. I got problems of my own."

"You mean you've changed your mind? You're going straight?"

I say nothing.

"I reckoned you might of had something once," he says. "But I guess you're just scared like the rest of us."

"Who said I was scared?"

"Or maybe reformed," he says sadly.

"Like hell," I say.

# twelve

THERE'S no more grog so we wander over to the counter, order a coke, and sit down at our table again.

"Had any fun since?" Jeff asks.

"No," I say. "The usual drag. I ran into a University mob, thought they might be O.K. but they were a worse fake than the bodgie gang—only rich enough to get away with it."

"Got any ideas?" he asks.

"Plenty," I lie. "Getting out of this city for a start. It gives me the shits."

"Me too," he says. "I'd like to get out and forget about this doll, but I don't know where. They reckon there's some work going in the wheatbelt over harvest, but I don't know about those parts."

I ask him where exactly and he says my home town.

"Yeah," I say. "It'd be swell to do a job there. Just swell."

"You'd know a few people there, I suppose?"

"Sure," I say. "Kindest, best meaning folks in the world, and all those lovely kids who bashed me up at school. Guess they'll be big men now. Big dumb farmers with dials like sheep and bellies full of wheat."

I feel the old hate rise up in me like a fanned fire.

107

"Kicked me out for my own good at nine years old. Set my feet firmly on the path to hell. Yeah, sure. I think the world of that little town and its folks with their big reputation for hospitality. Open house. Anything we got is yours, boy. Help yourself. They'd be tickled pink to welcome me back."

"Well, I guess that's out," Jeff says. "I thought if I'd found a mate I might have had a stab at it."

"You've found one," I say.

"What do you mean?"

"I often thought about going back to do a job there," I tell him. "Why not tonight?"

"You're crazy," he says. "It's about a hundred miles."

"Ninety eight. What's that in a flash new car?"

"Gee," he says. "You must be even drunker than you look."

"Come on, let's go."

"We can't."

"Why not?" I laugh. "Waiting for Godot?"

"Who?"

"Friend of mine," I say. "Literary acquaintance."

"We'd have to plan a thing like that real carefully," Jeff says.

"Listen man," I tell him, dropping my voice. "I had this thing planned in detail the last eighteen months. It was just a matter of choosing the time. All we need is a torch and a couple of tools."

"Sure," he says. "Except only a flash car."

"Little thing like that's no problem."

"I said I'd never come at that again. Not after last time."

"Look," I say. "I'm not pushing you into this. You don't want to come at it, O.K. But that last car job you did was a moron act. You deserved what was coming to you."

"Yeah," he agrees. "I made a silly mistake."

I get to my feet again. "O.K., man. Be seeing you some time."

"You going to pull it on your own?"

"Why not?" I fake it casual, but I need a mate to put this job through properly. If he won't come in I'll call it a night and go to bed. It just came all over me again, thinking of the old town, but I don't care much now anyway. I walk to the door and he follows me out into the street.

"What was the plan?" he asks.

"Pick up a car," I say. "Bust a store in this one horse town, then burn off out of the State. Start all over. New place. New life."

"Gee, it would be swell," he says. "Start all over. Clean sheet. No record hanging round your neck like a lump of concrete."

"What about the big doll?" I ask.

"She's a bitch," he says. "I feel ashamed of myself wanting her."

"Forget her," I say. "There's as many more bitches in the pound as ever came out of it."

"I could forget her all right if we cleared out. Where do we pick up the tools and the torch?"

He's real keen now and I guess I have to go through with it.

"I have an acquaintance round here," I say. "He'll lend us anything we want."

"Are you sure?" he asks. "This time of night?"

"Sure," I say. "Any time at all."

"Some pal," he says.

"Some pal," I agree. It's the same chap I borrowed the clothes from. He won't say "No" even if he wants to.

We get to the house. I go round the side and tap on his window. It is open and I can hear him breathing in his sleep, so I climb in and shake him awake. He sits up with a start and I put a hand over his mouth. "It's only me," I say. "Sorry it's like late, but I have to get a torch, a jemmy and a screw-driver. You've still got them, I guess."

"O.K.," he says, gets up and fumbles around in the dark. "You might let me have them back some time."

"Sure," I say, "with interest. Thanks man. Have to be getting on now. Seeing you!"

"Seeing you," he whispers. "Good luck."

Out in the street again we pass a few parked cars and give them a quick glance over. None of them are what I'm looking for. Not flash looking or fast enough. Outside the Salvation Army Citadel there is the sort of sleek, hot looking model I have in mind. A warlike Christian car. Like new. Good. I owe them a debt for the hymn bashing they bored me with in jail.

"Onward Christian soldiers!" I whisper.

No one about. We try the doors and find that the fools have even forgotten to lock up. It's a gift. We jump inside. It would be too much to expect them to have left the key, but who cares? We join the wires under the dashboard and the motor kicks to life.

I let Jeff take the wheel for the first lap. I have to do the thinking for this job and am so tense I would probably start speeding too soon and have the cops on us. Christ, now I've made up my mind to do this job, get out of the State, I want to put it through. I didn't care for a bit, but now I don't want to land up in can again.

Jeff drives well, reliable. Thirty-five to forty as the city lights move backwards on either side, fifty when the lights thin out. No speed cops to worry us here. Jeff presses his foot flat and the whispers of fear fade as we flash along. Free! Grey jail forgotten. Zoom!

We talk and laugh as the road winds on, the head-lights ripping a yellow path between the gums.

"Oh God, Our Father, lead us into money and deliver us from all policemen."

"Gee, she's a swell bomb, this," Jeff says. "Hope we can hang on to her. We could change the number plates, buy some paint and slap her over."

"No," I say. "We'd better ditch her in the scrub round Southern Cross. Kalgoorlie maybe. Word'll be in all the papers by that time. Should pick up another flash crate there—big mining executive job. Load a drum of petrol if possible. Service stations are a bad risk once the wires start buzzing."

"Gee, you think of everything," Jeff says.

"Yeah," I say. "Don't worry about this crate. Tear the guts out of her. Rip the rubber off the tyres. Who cares?"

I have a swell feeling of power now. Not a puny human weakling any more. Sort of god-like and the engine roaring out my strength at the world.

Arrow reflectors glow warnings of hidden bends. Wheels squeal and squawk around the curves. Steady, man. Even a god can die!

A glow erupts into a town. Street lights open up the roadsides. An all-night café and filling station flashes red neon letters and we pull to a stop. Chance to refuel while we have a quick coffee and something to eat. We crawl cramped from the seat, walk jerkily into the shop, order a snack and ask the attendant to fill the tank.

The steaming coffee and hamburgers let the tension down a bit but Jeff notices my hand shake as I light a cigarette.

"Feeling nervous?" he asks.

I say it's good to feel a bit that way—keeps the circulation toned up for action. The café clock says one a.m. No time to waste, but still I dawdle over my cigarette.

"Let's go," Jeff urges. "What are we waiting for?"

I glance from the bright lights, into the dark unknown outside. "Godot, I guess."

"Who did you say?"

"Nobody." . . . "In an instant all will vanish and we'll be alone again, in the midst of nothingness." . . . My grey mood has come over me again. All desire for action has gone from me.

"All right," I say. "Let's go."

We have only about enough between us to pay for the petrol and the meal, but Jeff is cheerful and confident. He is fool enough to believe in me.

"We're about half-way now," he says as we walk back to the car. "Your turn to take over."

# thirteen

WE start up again. I soon relax behind the wheel and begin to enjoy myself again. I have a sense of fusion with this machine and have to remind myself how I am always separate and alien from everything and everyone. No ties any more, not even to my mum. That was the hardest to break I guess, but nothing left now since the last time I was out.

Mum had come up from the wheatbelt and got herself a cheap furnished room not far out from Perth. I'd seen her there a couple of times before and she knew how it was going with me. She fussed over me at first and said how she could still make a home for me if I got a steady job, but I knew by this time. There was nothing she could do for me and precious little I could ever do for her except break any heart she had left. Last time out, she didn't even mention it any more. Loneliness hit me in the face as she opened the door and she looked hopeless and sick, but I didn't feel a thing. Did she expect me to thank her for bringing me into this stinking world? I guess she had a good time getting me—enough to pay my debt. . . .

"Good day, Mum. Just got out of bloody, stinking jail."

"I knew you were in, son," she says. "Making quite a name for yourself."

"How did you know?" I ask. "I thought they didn't publish the juvenile names."

"Your friend came and told me."

"What friend?"

"That pimply-faced boy."

"He's an acquaintance. I don't have any friends."

"I don't either, for that matter," she says. "It gets pretty lonely on my own. I came here after Mr Willy died because I thought I'd see you kids sometimes. Never see the others at all now. They're too good for their poor old mum."

Well, she never did that damn much for them and they never minded going away like I did that time. Jesus, she looks worn out though, and letting herself go, too. Straggly hair and sloppy old clothes. How soon can I get out of here? The stink of the old is worse than jail.

I went back to see her once more. Yes, after the car bust. Found those bags of coins in a briefcase at the back—pennies and two shilling bits.

"It's me again, Mum. Your son." She opens the door. "Got some pennies for you. Don't know how much. You can change them for silver if you like."

"Thanks, son. Always have a need for a few pennies. They do nicely for the gas."

I take the bags from my pockets and throw them on her bed.

114

"Nice of you to remember me, son. There's never much left of my pension after the rent."

I look at her. "You sick or something?" I ask.

"I've been in hospital," she says, "but I'm better now. A priest came to see me in there and I went to confession for the first time in years."

"Did you a lot of good, I s'pose?"

"Yes, son. I've felt better about things since. He was a nice priest and he said——"

"I have to go now, Mum. Got an appointment with a chick. See you again some time, Mum."

That means never. . . .

Now the road swings into my home town. We pull up quietly in a side street, rest and smoke a cigarette to calm our nerves. No lights and nothing moving in the dark.

"O.K.," I say. "Better get on with it."

An eerie sound breaks the stillness and we freeze beside the car. I hear the heavy flop of wings and glance up as the dark shape of a mopoke blurs the sky. The cold eyes of the stars compel me to look into them and fill me with a terrible doubt. Up to this everything I have done and planned to do seemed just and right, but now suddenly for some reason it seems all wrong. There is no right and wrong, I remind myself. I found that out long ago. It's only a trick to keep the squares on top. I glance at Jeff, expecting he's feeling the same way and will suggest calling it off. I could despise him then and it would let me out. But he has butted his cigarette and picked up the jemmy from the seat. He is too dumb to change his mind at this stage. He thinks it will be all right because I have told him so.

I've already decided to start on the hardware store on the corner, and I lead the way, hunching along in my cat walk. Chunky farm machinery bulks in the dark of the veranda as we make for the gates in the side street. Behind them is a yard where I remember oil and petrol drums were stored, and there are the same five-foot gates, iron frames covered with wire mesh, chained together and padlocked.

We climb up easily, but the gates rattle as we jump down into the drum-filled yard. We crouch until silence falls again, then slip through the yard to the shop. Everything is the same except the wire-netting that now encloses the back veranda. This is bad. No wire cutters. I feel around and find a small door, but it is padlocked fast. I slip the jemmy into the curve of the lock and jerk. It grates but holds firm. I try again. A few more quick jerks and the lock springs open with a snap, falls, and clangs against a piece of metal underneath. The noise seems loud enough to wake the dead and we stand hardly daring to breathe. Nothing moves, so I push the door and we ooze through to the dark veranda.

The flashlight reveals heaps of junk—a rusty forged iron plough and odd parts of agricultural implements. Behind them is a window leading into the shop. I take the torch and hand the jemmy to Jeff. "Try and lever it up." He slips a wedge end under the sash. The old lock squeaks and twists and the frame rises to make a fingerhold. Good. I lift the window cautiously. The inside gapes like a toothless mouth and we wriggle through, feet first. Jeff takes the torch, puts the jemmy in his belt, and cups the beam in his hand.

I search quickly in the shrouded gleam for anything that might hold cash. No luck yet, but I find a rack of rifles, pick up a .22 calibre and a box of ammunition. I unclip the eight shot magazine and press in the slug. Like feeding a baby. Fine. With the weight of a weapon in my hand I feel secure and confident.

We find an unlocked door and enter noiselessly. It is an office. Lucky break. We pull out drawers and toss out files. No money. I try the desk. The locked drawer must be where they keep the lolly. The jemmy bursts it easily and the cash box inside is not even locked. We stuff notes and coins into our pockets. Plenty time later to share it out. Nothing else here worth taking except the rifle, and I have that.

"Right," I whisper. "Let's go."

Back in the yard again, and a faint noise resolves itself into the heavy tread of boots. Only one set of footsteps, but coming down hard and solid, echoing purpose and authority. Clump, clump. Pause. The rattle of a chain and the snap of a padlock.

"Hell! Sounds like a cop."

We dare not use the torch as we dash across the yard towards the stack of stuff we noticed on the way in. I kick a tin as I dive for shelter and the noise echoes through the night like a thunderclap. The footsteps slow down and stop and a powerful flash-beam roves the yard probing into the darkest corners among the stack of oil drums. I'm real scared now, as the light moves mercilessly towards our hiding-place. Sweat-scared.

In seconds endless vistas of grey jail memories pass through my mind. Bleak greyness of prison walls, sterile white of the square cells, cold grey light of the corridors, dreary, grey drag of the long days. God how I struggled to harden my spirit to its misery. Told myself I didn't care any more. It didn't make much difference where I was—one place much like another—all dreary and all a drag. Prison a refuge of a sort where I was nearer belonging than anywhere. But now in these crazy two days I have felt the sun again and seen the sky and breathed the fresh, sweet air. Does it have to be over again so soon? Must I just wait and take it like before? Why should I, when I have this power in my hands? None of them ever spared me. Why should I spare one of them? I fumble in the dark with the bolt of the rifle and a bullet clicks sharply into place. The torch beam swings and slaps me full in the face. I blink and panic and the rifle explodes with a crack of doom into the blinding light. The weapon leaps in my hand. A short exclamation of surprise or pain, a heavy thud and the light blacks out.

Mind screams "Run, run, run", but I crouch petrified. I hear a sobbing whisper in my ear as Jeff leaps from hiding and runs past to the gate. "Hurry. Get the bloody hell out of here."

I spring into action and scramble after him. Lights flash on in house windows along the street where we have left the car. Jeff is heading that way. He doesn't know the layout of this place and is making into a trap. I turn the other way, across the railway line, past the shadowy goodsheds and the big wheat silo, silvery grey in the starlight, past the stock pens and into the dark refuge of the bush. Heart pounding, breath a ragged gasping of air, I am clutching my rifle for dear life. So dear, dear life.

A mile or so now between my fear and the town, and after stumbling and falling through the scrubby undergrowth my eyes have grown more accustomed to the dark. I see that I have come on some wheel tracks. I stop and take my bearings. The town that way. This way, two, three miles on, should be the hill I used to climb. This must be the little track old Mr Willy made with his horse and dray.

Small sounds of waking birds drop sharply into the massive silence as I flip flop between the tortured limbs of paperbarks and the ghost-stark trunks of the gums.

What will it be this time if they catch up with me? Hanging for sure. If I killed that cop. Or life. Hanging would be better. Quick short drop to everlasting void. Not peace. Just nothingness. I reason with myself, but terror takes me by the throat and my knees go weak.

A sharp stick finger jabs my cheek and I let out a yelp of pain. It acts as a stimulus to my fear-numbed brain and steadies my nerves. I feel the blood trickling down my cheek, wipe it away with my sleeve and keep on walking, feet feeling out the narrow strip of saneness through the crazed bush.

# fourteen

A FIRST grey glow of dawn spreads from the horizon
and out through the bush. A shadow moves from the
shadow of a tree. My rifle springs up defensively.
Reason tells me it is a kangaroo, instinct that it is a
man.. I release the safety catch, stop dead and wait.
A terrible tiredness has come over me, leaving me
drained of all power to feel or act. The shadow comes
quietly, soundlessly, on along the sandy track. A man
or the ghost of a man stops a few yards from me. I
stand dead still in my black clothes against the blackened bole of a tree, but I sense that eyes are feeling
me out, feature for feature, limb for limb.

"You look done in, boy." An old voice, deep and
soft—not a white man's voice. "No good to feel that
way."

"I got lost," I say. "Been walking all night."

"You need a spell," he says. "I got a camp over
there."

Too right I need a spell, but dare I take the risk?
What the hell. He can't know who I am or what I've
done and, anyway, he's so old. I follow him off the

track into the bush until the glow of a fire marks the camp in a clearing near the foot of the big hill. There is a lean-to that seems to be made of branches, paper-bark and hessian bags, and over the fire, suspended between forked sticks, hangs a steaming billycan. The old man leans to stir the coals, and I see that he is a thoroughbred—not mongrel like me. A thick mop of white hair throws up the blackness of his lined face. The skin of his hands is cracked with age, the hands themselves, long fingered, supple, almost delicate. His bare, dusty feet are stumpy and look tough as leather. Something about him twangs a chord of memory. Where have I seen him before, what do I know of him?

"Sit down," he says. "I get you a feed first and you can sleep."

He comes out from the shelter with a metal plate and spoon, stirs the billy and ladles food onto the plate. I'm starving and the stew is good. I wolf it down.

"Jessie Duggan's boy," he says, like talking to himself.

The food sticks in my throat. "No," I say. "I'm a stranger here."

"You're in trouble, son."

"I come out after kangaroo," I say, "and I get lost. That's all."

"I known your mummie and your grandmummie. That old woman, she been my tribal sister you know. She call me brother, only your mummie can't call me uncle any more. She got to forget all that in the mission school."

I look at the broad, black face in the growing daylight and memory sounds a clear note. The old rabbiter who used to come to our house sometimes—the
one my mother warned me about. A bit crazy and
might be dangerous, she said, and I was never to talk
to him. He must be the one the kids said was a magic
man who talked the language of the bush animals.
But that seems a lifetime ago. Fancy him still around.
He doesn't look dangerous now and probably never
was. I expect it was just this tribal relative idea of his
that worried Mum. Maybe it was even true, but that
side of my heritage must be kept from me at all costs.
I must live white and learn to think with a white
man's mind.

He sits in the swelling daylight and nods at me
quietly across the fire. I finish eating and put the plate
on the ground. "Thanks," I say. "I've got to get going
now."

He does not seem to have heard this.

"Long time you don't see her, son," he says.

"Who?"

"Your old mummie."

I feel a sudden prick of shame. "No, she lives in the
city now. I can't get there much."

He shakes his head quietly.

"She come back here."

"To this town?"

"That Noongar camp, close up."

"Mum in the Noongar camp?"

"She got nobody, only them, son. They look after
her all right, but I think she die soon."

I push from my mind the thought of the squalid

shacks, slapped together from bits and pieces off the rubbish dumps, the dirt floors and the leaking roofs—aching hot in summer, cold and wet in the winter's rain—Mum with her fastidious ways lying on filthy blankets and old bags. Mum, with her phoney pride, dependent on the kindness of the people she reared me to despise. The Noongar mob, shiftless and hopeless, but with a sort of strength, a blood call to their kind that she knew and feared.

So now she has gone back to die with them and be buried in that back part of the cemetery in a nameless Noongar grave. Serve her right. She had it coming to her, pretending to be better than the rest of them, keeping me away from them, giving me over like a sacrificial offering to the vicious gods of the white man's world. The Noongars have their vices all right. They take their sex like they take their grog—wherever and whenever it comes along. They brawl and bash each other up, gamble the shirts off their backs and make fools of anyone who tries to help them, but they have a warmth and loyalty to each other and a sort of philosophy of life the whites will never know or understand. We would both have been better off if we had stuck with them.

Well, no use pretending any more with this old bloke. He knows me, and all about me probably, except this latest episode. He takes a blanket that has been spread on the slope of his humpy, and offers it to me.

"Go in there now, son," he says. "Have a good sleep now."

His face is furrowed but simple and calm. No madness there. No sign of bitterness or the shifty look of the old black cadgers who hang around the country towns. I don't know what sort of a relative he thinks he is, but it means something to him and I guess he won't give me away. I take the blanket and curl up on the ground inside the hut. . . .

Falling, falling. Plunging and twisting out of the sky. Down and down and the dark ground rising up. . . .

I wake with a pounding heart and sit bolt upright, remembering. I've got to face the day and this hole I'm in. Can't stay here and talk to a crazy old nigger with all the cops in the district combing the bush for me. Got to get up and move on. I've killed a cop back there and I'm in for it if I don't think clear and act shrewd. Get my bearings and head East. Pinch another car if I can and get out of the State. I can lose myself over East. Grow a beard. Dress differently. No mercy for a man who kills a cop. I'm not sorry for him. All cops deserve to die, but most people don't see it that way and the world's going to be more against me now than it ever was.

I look around the hut. On an upturned box there is a battered pannikin, a couple of spoons, a butcher's knife and a cracked cup containing a few shillings. I put my head outside and look around, blinking in the white glare of the mid-day sun. No sign of the old man. The old bastard's probably gone to put me in. I was a fool to trust him. Should have remembered you can't trust anyone.

I take the money out of the cup and put it in my pocket. I've got all this other cash from the job at the hardware store, but I'm going to need all I can get, and more. My hand hovers over the knife. I hear a sound and look outside again. The old codger's coming back alone across the clearing, dangling some rabbits on a stick and droning his dreary blackman's song. It gets on my nerves. I drop the knife and put my hands over my ears.

He walks slowly to the fire, puts down the rabbits and peers into the hut. "Just been to the traps," he says. "Fresh meat for dinner now."

I crawl out and get on my feet.

"I'm on my way."

I think he's going to ask me "Where?" but he just nods and says, "You got a long way to go, son. Better eat while you got the chance."

I look at the limp, furry bodies by the fire. "No time," I say.

He goes to the billy, sniffs it, nods and tips the contents on a plate. I eat standing up while he reaches into the hut for his knife and begins to skin his catch. I put the plate down and he smiles at me again. "Wait a tick," he says, getting to his feet. "I got a few bob here put by. You might be glad of it."

I stand rooted to the spot until he returns with the empty cup in his hands. He looks at me quietly and I feel he is reading my whole life from my face. Everything, as long back as I can remember, even before. So what? I tell myself. What do I care for an old abo crank in beggar's clothes?

I look him straight in the face with my practised sneer. His eyes are faded like potch opal, but clear and sad. Not judging me, only seeing how I am. I feel the blood flushing up my neck and over my face and I hang my head. No one ever made me feel this way before. No one. Not the magistrate, or the probation officer, or the brothers with all that thunder about the eye of God. Not even my Mum's suffering face.

I take the money from my pocket and drop it back in the cup.

He shakes his head. "You take it, son. I don't have much use for it."

He puts the cup on the ground, then sits cross-legged and goes quietly on with his job. I want to run and hide my shame in the bush, but something holds me here. He begins to sing again, softly, like the humming of a bee, then the words shape on his lips and he breaks off.

"You know that song, son."

"Suppose I heard it somewhere before," I say.

"You dream it," he says. "It belong your country."

"I haven't got a country," I say. "I don't belong anywhere."

"You can't lose it," he says. "You go away, but you keep it here." He claps his hands under his ribs. "Inside. You dream that place and that song too. I hear you sing it in your sleep."

"I have a dream," I say, "but I don't remember when I wake up. A sort of falling dream."

"Might be your granny teach it when you been a little fella. Desert country." He makes a pointing motion with his chin.

"I don't remember any grandmother."

"Good woman," he says, "properly blackfella. No white blood."

"You knew her?" I ask.

"My sister," he says simply. He nods. "She give you that song might be."

I want to go, but something holds me here.

"What does it mean, anyway?"

"Belong dreaming time," he says. "That cat want to live a long time like the old crow. 'How you don't die?' he asks. 'I fly up high, high up to the moon. I get young up there, then come down.' That cat look sorry then. 'I got no wings.' Then the old crow laugh carr-carr. 'You don't need no wings. You can fly all right. You try now.' See?"

The old voice trails on, but now I have remembered the dream. It has been in some secret part of my mind to which he has given me the key.

In it I somehow play both parts, and I am also the spectator. I feel the sudden surprised wonder of flight —a trick of some leg muscle, as though rediscovered from a past bird life. I soar into the air with my cat body and my crow's wings, up and up. Almost there. Almost. Don't look down. Keep your cat-crow eyes on the swelling, bright face of the moon. Not down. Not down. But the old earth is pulling you. Got to look down. Crow laughs and cat hates. He has been deceived. It is a trick. Have to have wings to reach the moon. . . . Crow laughing, car-carr-carrr. . . . Wild cat plunging downwards through the night with terror in its glazed cat eyes. I am watching and the terror is my own. I am the crow laughing to see such fun. It is I falling, falling, plunging to my certain doom. I wake with the doom pounding at my heart.

The dream remembered and some long ago reality of a childhood fall—a slip knot giving way from round the high branch of a tree—falling, falling to oblivion. Don't remember hitting the ground. Only the fear and then the waking up with a bandage round my head. Why did I have to wake? Why must the old man recall for me this terrible foreshadowing?

The urgency of my plight comes over me afresh.

"Thanks for the food and everything. I have to go now."

He dives into his hut and brings out the rifle. I look at it in his outstretched hand. I've got a few slugs in my pocket, but I don't see myself using it now. Only something to carry.

"You can keep it," I say.

He shakes his head. "It only make trouble for me. I got no gun licence you know." He looks at me steadily. "Might make trouble for you, too."

"It's done that already."

I take the rifle from his hand. I don't want to kill anyone else, but if it comes to the point I might need it for myself. Better to end the nightmare that way.

"Wait," he says. "You want some water this time of year." He hitches the strap of his canvas bag over my shoulder. "I got a spare somewhere. Fill it up every chance you get."

I nod. "Which way's East?"

He motions again with his chin. "Take that old track," he says, and puts a hand on my arm as I turn to go. "This country knows you all right, son. You keep to the bush."

At a turn in the track I glance back and lift a hand. The old man is bent to his task again, but the comforting melancholy of his chant reaches out to me as I hurry on.

I don't know where the track is leading, but the bush seems more friendly now. I think how part of me once hunted in this forest of gums and banksias, how I was naked then and swung easily along with my light bundle of spears and boomerangs and the heart inside of me light and free. These clothes I have on are heavy-hot, but I am too soft to throw them away. The water-bag and the rifle are heavy, too, and my feet have no spring in them.

There is a dusty tang of eucalypts and a faint drift of smoke. High summer rings through the hot afternoon. Cicadas and sharp bird notes and a fitful wind among thin leaves and brittle grass. And under it all like the beat of a pulse, the old man's song. It could not carry this far, but he has sung it into my mind for as long as I have left to live.

In the yellow sand of the track ahead a stumpy tail lizard lies inert. I pause for breath and look at it, scaly and fat, its head wedge-shaped, its legs stunted and absurd. It turns, huffs defiance, and flickers out its long blue tongue at me.

"Sorry, brother," I say and step carefully over it. It is a sort of apology to all the lizards I ever tortured with sticks as a kid, perhaps to all the bush and its creatures for my indifference.

The wind drops suddenly and the cicada note stops

dead. I am the only living thing stirring in the bush. I long to rest but my fear drives me on through the furnace heat. I dare not drink more than a sip or two from the canvas bag, for God knows where I will find water in this summer dry wilderness. The country may know me as the old man says, but it does not tell me this.

The bark of a dog breaks the eerie silence. I stop in my tracks, alert. The sound comes from behind. Closer, until now I hear the unmistakable sound of horses' hooves. Run! Get in behind those rocks. Hide in a tree. . . . What's the use? If it's the police, the dogs will smell me out.

I sit down beside the track, the rifle in my hand. Have I the guts to end it here? Why not? There's no hope for me. No future except at the end of a rope. I have told myself so often that I want to die, but I guess it wasn't really true. I've always wanted to live. It was just the God-damn way life always went for me made me decide it was futile and absurd. I tried to stamp out any hope I had in me, but I never really killed it. It wouldn't die. And now when there's nothing to look forward to but the long-drawn-out misery of trial and punishment, I want to live more than I ever knew before. I even feel I might know just a little how to live.

Only yesterday I would have wanted to shoot it out like the big shot movie boys and become a sort of posthumous hero to the gang. Ned Kelly in bodgie dress; but I feel different now. Like I was somebody else. Before I've always tried to run away. Why not stick around and face up to something for a change?

Great thoughts. Swell sentiments. I guess it only means I haven't got the guts to kill myself. I throw the rifle from me with all my strength.

The dogs come first, they leap and yelp around me as I stand against a tree like a cornered kangaroo. Sharp teeth clamp on my trouser leg and rip my skin. I am real scared now. Almost glad when the horsemen show up and call them off. One of them walks up to me and shows his badge. He asks my name and charges me with attempted murder.

The meaning takes a while to register. Attempted murder. Attempted. I haven't killed him then. Relief surges and recedes. But he might still die. . . .

"How bad is he?" I ask.

"Bad enough."

"Is he going to live? I didn't mean to kill a man. It wasn't in my mind."

The copper is tall with a stern face. He looks at me and I look back at him. I have never found or expected any kindness or pity in a copper's face. Is it possible there is a hint of humanity in this man's eyes? And why now when I have done the worst thing in my life?

"He'll live," he says, and snaps the cuffs on my unresisting hands.